P9-EDR-026

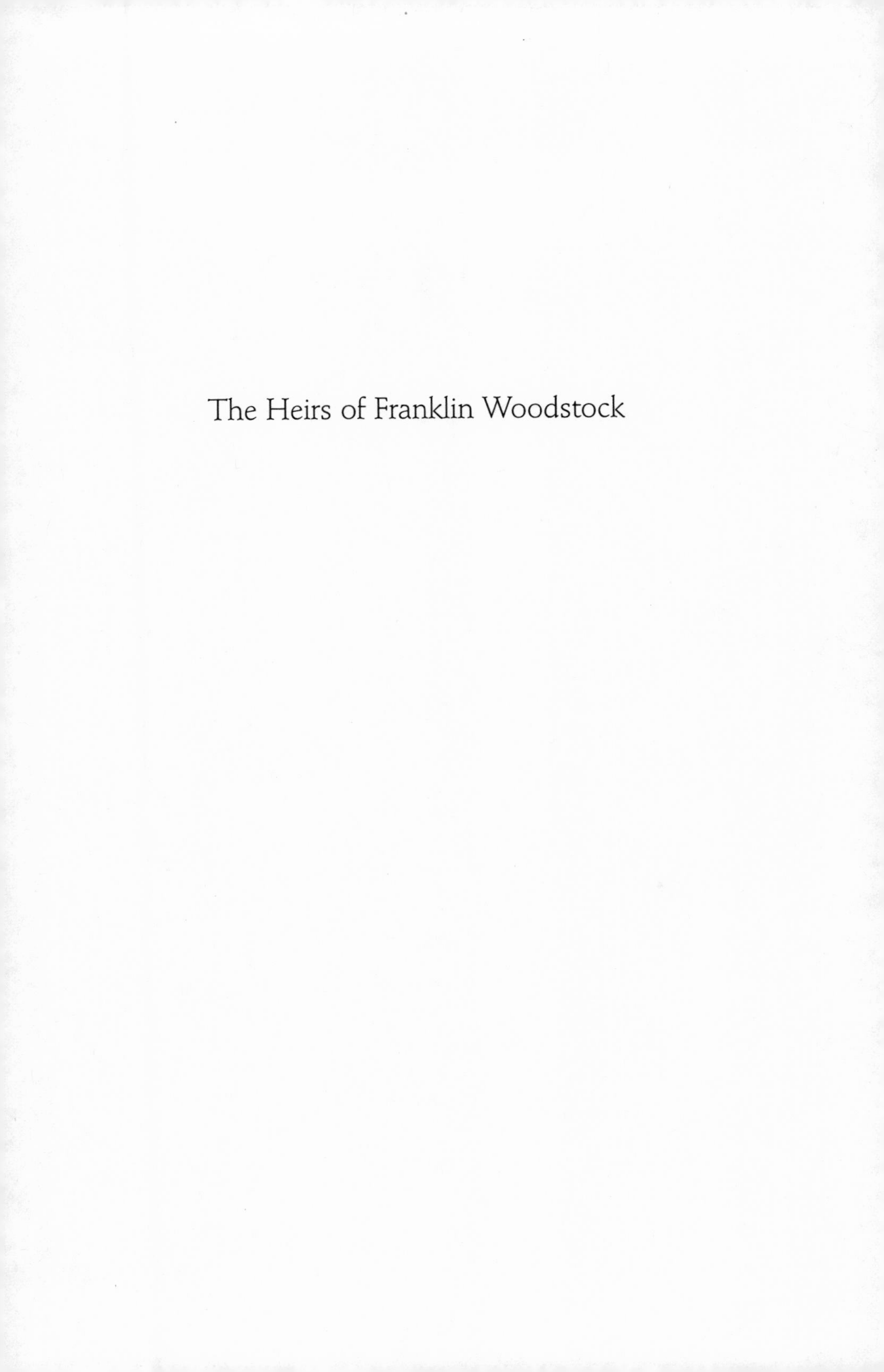

The Heirs of Franklin Woodstock

Benjamin Capps

THE HEIRS OF Franklin Woodstock

Texas Christian University Press
Fort Worth

Library of Congress Cataloging-in-Publication Data

Capps, Benjamin, 1922–
The heirs of Franklin Woodstock : a novel / by Benjamin Capps.
p. cm.
ISBN 0-87565-036-8
I. Title.
PS3553.A59H4 1989
813'.54—dc19 88-39269
CIP

Designed by Whitehead & Whitehead

Contents

Dedicated to
My son, Mark V. Capps

CHAPTER ONE

Escape

George Woodstock received the peculiar phone call on his sixty-sixth birthday. He had been at the machine shop since seven, getting his three employees set up for the day's work and planning what to ask a toolmaker who was applying for a job and was supposed to come in at eleven for an interview. His wife Helen had proposed that George stay home and take her out to lunch and a shopping spree to celebrate his birthday, but he had declined.

He let the phone ring twice, then answered, "Woodstock Machine Shop."

It was Helen's voice. "Clara called, George."

"Where is she?"

"Your sister. She's out at Woodstock where she always is. Your papa has escaped from the nursing home."

He waited a full five seconds.

"George? Do you hear?"

"Helen, is this you? Will you please explain what you're talking about? Escaped?"

"That's what Clara said. That's her words."

"What in the hell does *escaped* mean? Did you ask any questions? Did you talk to Ed? Have they put up a fence for patients to climb over? Or did he tunnel out? Did he wound any guards? I thought Papa was in a nursing care facility."

"Please don't be snotty, George. I'm only telling you what Clara said. I said you'd call back."

"Clara is a dingbat. Always has been. If you didn't talk to Ed, you don't know what happened. I'll call Ed. Do you know if he'll be at home or at the hardware store or out at the ranch?"

"No."

"I'll call him when I can and try to make a little sense out of it. I'll call him right after lunch."

"And, George?"

"Can you come by K-Mart and bring me some bags for the vacuum?"

"Honey, I've got nineteen things on my mind. Can't you drive over there?"

She said, "Okay."

He felt put upon by such an emergency and realized that there was a selfish, personal thing in it. He did not want to be beyond middle age, had too much at stake in the shop to admit that he might start getting old. As long as the old man was ninety-one and still going strong, his own birthdays did not matter. Like a crazy little prayer, he thought: *Get on the ball, Papa. Don't do foolish things.*

The office of Woodstock Machine Shop was a twelve by twelve room partitioned off in one corner of the large metal-covered building. Crowded into the office were a drafting table with a shaded fluorescent light hanging over it, a metal desk littered with papers, two chairs, two filing cabinets, his own tool chests stacked in one corner. The concrete floor had not been swept for a month. He made a few notes on the yellow legal pad for the interview, glad to have some important duty to take his mind off of his father.

The toolmaker who had called in answer to the newspaper ad came in exactly at eleven. He looked fortyish, neat in khakis, said his name was Robert Fowler. He was stout of build, had a small grin.

When they were seated, George said, "Mr. Fowler, if you

like the looks of that shop out there, I can't use you. We don't have the space and machinery for a good job shop."

They laughed and George said, "More about that later. We are going to expand. Now, I believe you said you have had twenty-one years experience. Whereabouts?"

"LTV, TI, Conso, a couple of small shops. It's twenty-one years if you count one hitch in the Navy. I worked as an apprentice machinist at San Diego and aboard ship. That's where I got my start."

"Do you consider yourself an A-class tool and die maker?"

"Sure." The small grin came out.

George could not quite figure out what the small grin meant. He noted with approval that the man's fingernails had been cleaned but still had traces of grease under them.

"What personal tools do you have, Bob? We don't have a toolroom around here."

"Oh, mikes up to six inches. Inside mikes. Depth mikes. A couple of master squares. Couple of indicators. Transfer punches and screws. That kind of stuff. Tooling ball. Edge finder. Adjustable parallels. Small sine bar. I don't know. I've got a Gerstner box like that one in the corner and another box for rough tools. They're both full."

"Do you have any cutting tools?"

"Fraction drills up to a half. Letter drills. Number drills. Reamers to a half. Counter borers. I've got taps, maybe half a set, coarse and fine, up to five-eighths. Some end mills. Stuff like that."

George had decided that the man would do for a trial. Now, as he turned his thoughts to a justification of the offer he was about to make, he could not keep his mind from flashing momentarily back and forth to the "escape" of his father.

"Bob, I have the promise of some financing and we are going to enlarge this place and get some better machine tools. We hope to do it within a year. I can pay you twelve bucks an hour right now. You'll be on trial, and Woodstock Machine Shop will be on trial. I need five A-class toolmakers, counting myself, and we will own this place as equal partners. The five have to be top-notch, no bluffing. One or two could be general machinists instead of bench men. How does that sound?"

"Well, Mr. Woodstock, how would I buy in?"

He was thinking, *I hope to the devil I don't have to go to West Texas right now. Surely Ed Bender would be able to make some sense out of the "escape."*

"We will work that out when we come to it. If you start now, you don't obligate yourself to anything. In other words, if you don't like the proposition, you can say no. But it's a chance don't many men get that work for wages."

"Well, Mr. Woodstock. I saw three guys already working out there. What . . .?"

"They won't be partners. When we get going like I hope, we'll have maybe ten workers that draw good wages and do just what they're told. The five of us, we make the tools and set them up and they produce. But my plan is that all five of us that are owners, including me, get our hands dirty. If you know what I mean."

The smile on the face of Robert Fowler made him look dubious, but he said, "I'd like to give it a whirl."

"Can you bring your boxes in tomorrow?"

"Sure. What time?"

"You can come in at seven or eight. No time clock. Just put in forty hours. I'll be here to get you started on something."

After the fellow left, George saw that it was only 11:30 and debated whether to make the long distance call from the shop or go home. With a slight prick of guilt, he decided that it was a business expense. What the hell. Even though it was his father, it was connected with getting the financing so that he could make a strong, going concern out of the shop: and that would make money for IRS as well as everybody else.

He walked down two blocks to the main drag and bought a large hamburger at the McDonald's and a six-pack of Pearl beer at the convenience store. Back at the shop he put five cans of the beer in the Pontiac and took the other in to drink with the hamburger. One of the hands said, "Hey, Woodstock, if you aim to get drunk, we won't have to work very hard this afternoon."

"That's where you're wrong. I work people twice as hard when I'm drunk." Then he added, "There is no objection if anybody working for me wants to drink one beer during the noon break."

It was two o'clock before he finally got his nephew, Ed Bender, on the phone in the West Texas town of Woodstock. Ed sounded distraught, not like his usual businesslike self. He was at the hardware store.

"I guess he just walked off, Uncle George. About twelve o'clock midnight last night."

"Well, what is everybody doing? Business as usual?"

"I've been out to the ranch. Izzy and Johnny haven't seen him. The law people have put out a missing person deal. The people at the nursing home are no help; in fact they are nasty about it. Uncle George, I need some help out here."

"I don't see why, Ed. He could not have got very far. Where could he have gone? Did he have any help, or . . .?"

"That's it," Ed said. "Where? Johnny is out on horseback right now, looking every place he can figure. I thought about calling Uncle Walter. I've got to have some help. I can't get diddly-poop out of those nurses."

"Don't call Walter," he said. "I'll be out there tomorrow. Ask around town, will you?"

That was the way everything seemed to be these days; if you want something done in a responsible way, do it yourself. Or make it simple for someone else, then watch them like a hawk to see that it's done right. He could imagine his father, ninety-one years old, lying in a ditch somewhere, helpless. If the old man was stubborn, he had a right to be at his age. The old coot had earned the right to decent care even if he had become hard to get along with. Damn! The younger generation did not seem to have the concern that people used to have.

He locked up and went home at five. Helen had TV dinners in the oven. He was not in the mood for the news or much of anything else. He was full of questions and kept repeating the obvious, as did Helen: "Papa could not have gone far! Why can't they find him?"

She was really concerned. He said, "I trust Johnny out on the ranch, but no telling what kind of people they have at the nursing home or the sheriff's office. You want to go out there with me in the morning? It's nearly a three-hour drive."

"I can't. Tomorrow is my volunteer day for the Goodwill donation trailer at Skaggs parking lot. I hope it's a false alarm. Papa is too old to be out by himself. You'll find him."

She was always volunteering for something—working for the Salvation Army or Goodwill or baking cookies for a local Scout troop.

The following morning he got packed and drove to the shop early to miss the rush traffic. The new man, Bob Fowler, came in at seven. George got him set up on a work bench beside the office cubicle, where he could hear the phone. It was a touchy business to put him in charge of the shop on his first day, but necessary. He could sharpen a drill free-hand, which the others could not do. He did not seem intimidated by the prospect of figuring bend allowances and developing flat patterns from an engineering print, nor of sketching some plans for form blocks.

George considered whether his own hand tools might be needed while he was gone. His personal tools were precious to him. Finally he told the new man, "Get into my tool boxes if you need to. I'll try to get back tomorrow or call. I may wind up going to a funeral. I'll call."

"Okay, Mr. Woodstock."

It was nearly nine when he nosed the Pontiac west. He had missed the going-to-work rush and now had to fight only the bankers and salesmen and big trucks. He took the interstate around Fort Worth and, as usual, cursed the idiots who had written and designed and placed the highway signs. The world seemed to get more hectic all the time, more full of incompetent fools. Arrows pointing every which way, go this way, go that way. It was not because he was sixty-six; he felt just like he had at fifty-six. It was that the damned world was changing. It did not seem improper that New York or Chicago or Dallas or L.A. should have traffic problems. But Fort Worth? Mixmaster interchanges? Arrows pointing every which way? Go north in order to go west? Go east in order to go south? In Fort Worth? What was the world coming to? It did seem sometimes that not only the young rebels but the so-called Establishment just tried to make things as hectic as possible.

When he lined out west, the highway was nearly clear. It was a pleasure to drive a good, functioning machine on a good, clear highway. It was April, a late spring. The wild flowers were rampant in the outrageous colors of Indian paintbrush, of bluebonnets, sweet peas, tender yellow buttercups, crisp yellow dandelions. They stretched in great sweeps along the prairie and hills, as if scattered by a giant god. The hectic nature of life receded as he drove. Though Woodstock had not been his home for over forty-five years, he had the feeling of going home.

He had speculated about moving the shop to a less congested region, to Wichita Falls or Abilene, even Lubbock. The trouble was that he had the contacts where he was now and knew that he could get the work to keep a job shop busy. And it was important that he make a success out of his plan, just to prove himself right. Now with the kids well established in their own lives, he and Helen had enough to get by on, even travel around in a camper or such. Go fishing. Hell, he could even go on Social Security. But that kind of thing was impossible. It was almost as if he had a solemn pact with the old man, his father, based on a mutual understanding—one should become competent, no bluffing, at some important work, then use grand ideas to exploit that competence. He knew he could do it—become a pioneer in a new job shop system.

Now, easing along between fifty-five and sixty on the open highway, he thought about his one-two-three blocks, as he often did when he was alone for a few hours. They were blocks of hardened and ground steel, lightened by a pattern of holes, the blocks measuring one inch by two inches by three inches. Four mated blocks, useful for measurement and set-ups and layouts. He had made them on his own time over a period of years. For flatness, for parallel surfaces, for ninety degree corners, for dimensions, they were all within two-tenths of a thousandth of an inch. It had taken some lapping and polishing after surface grinding.

Although he had never got the chance to explain it to anyone, he had worked out an illustration to explain what a tenth of a thousandth is. Suppose a ream of typing paper, 500 pages, is two inches thick. Then there are 250 sheets in an inch. That means that each sheet is four thousandths of an inch or forty tenths. When you are talking about a tenth, you are talking about one-fortieth of the thickness of a piece of paper. Carpenters think measuring to a sixteenth is close enough; there are sixty-two and a half thousandths in a sixteenth, or six-hundred and twenty-five tenths.

If he did not use the one-two-three blocks for a few weeks, he would take them out of his box and wipe them off carefully with a lightly oiled cloth. They were a symbol. It's important to be accurate. An error in a toolmaker's tools is magnified in the production tooling he makes, then is magnified a lot more in the final manufactured product. And there are more and more shoddy products all the time.

The old man, Franklin Woodstock, his father, had understood all that, the pride and the reason for it. The last time they had talked—it was out at the ranch about a year ago—Papa had committed himself to an investment of a hundred thousand bucks with no strings, as soon as he, George, was ready to use it. A hundred thousand would be like seed money; with it invested in machinery, a bank would lend you any more you needed.

As he drove, a prick of guilt kept returning. He selfishly wanted Papa to live because of the investment commitment, to which there were no witnesses. But it wasn't true. He wanted the old man to live to see, to understand, what he had been doing as a surveyor, a navigator, a tool and die maker. To have in common with Papa the pride vindicated. As for the money, it was probably there, will or no will, but it would not be the same without the old man to see and understand. Above all right now he did not want the old man to be in pain or to feel alone and abandoned.

Going west from the Metroplex was like going into another world. Or going back in time. The land had changed, but not much. Above all, going west meant leaving behind the bustle and hurry and crowding. A person ought to be able to find peace out here.

The county-seat town of Woodstock had about three thousand population. He circled the courthouse square and parked in front of the hardware store. There were always empty parking places on the east side of the square. His nephew, Ed Bender, had a crude sign in the front window: SALE. FIX UP FOR SPRING. He also still had that idiot bell which rings when you go in the front door.

Ed was a roly-poly middle-aged man who wore suspenders. He came from the back of the poorly-lighted store, peering through his spectacles. "Uncle George! Am I glad to see you."

"Any news lately?"

"Nothing. Not a thing. Those people in the office at the nursing home are impossible to get anything out of. I guess it would be better to talk to the exact nurses that have been taking care of him."

"Been in touch with the ranch?"

"Johnny called early. He's still searching. That crazy son of mine, Homer, is out there to help, for whatever it's worth."

"Have you talked to people around town?"

"I am run ragged, Uncle George. I'm working on my income tax and it's driving me crazy. I don't have any help in this store except on Saturdays. I got six calls this morning, people wanting to know do I have any onion sets. What is a hardware store doing carrying onion sets? It's too late for green onions anyway."

He could see that Ed was in no mood to give him any help. "Well, I'll walk around town, Ed."

"If you get time I wish you would help me with my income tax. You were always good at arithmetic, Uncle George. I've got about eleven hundred bills and cancelled checks and receipts and stuff I don't even know what it is. And these CPAs want a small fortune for a couple of days work. And my calculator has gone on the blink."

"Afraid I can't help you. I've gone on the blink myself as far as IRS forms go."

"One thing I ought to tell you, Uncle George. You said don't call Uncle Walter. I guess Mother called him."

"Why?"

"Well . . . I suppose she figured he's the oldest."

"I didn't want to bother him till we know something, but I guess all the kids have got to be told. They have a right to know what's going on. If you see Clara before I do, tell her I think she should call Clarence and Irma."

"Okay, Uncle George."

He left the Pontiac parked where it was and walked around the courthouse square to the bank. It was a one-story brick building, which proudly announced in the masonry above the canvas awning: Established 1899.

He sat in the waiting area only a few minutes before a well dressed man came out of an office and called, "George Woodstock, hello." He knew he was supposed to know the man, a vice-president or something. Names escaped him these days.

Seated in the office, the banker asked, "How can we help you, Mr. Woodstock?"

"I would like to have a little information about my father's account."

"Sure. Certainly. There is a rumor going around town. I hope nothing serious has happened."

"He's just missing. That's all we know. I'm trying to get any facts I can. Do you have any way of knowing how much money Papa had? Available, I mean. Have any checks cleared?"

"Oh, we have not seen a check signed by him in months. Now, cash? Who knows? I've seen Franklin Woodstock walk out that front door many times with several thousand dollars in his hip pocket. He always paid his hands in cash. He made deals with cash. Who knows how much money he had out at the ranch or in his pocket or stashed somewhere? He could have had bank accounts in other towns for all we know."

"How are the affairs at the ranch handled? You say he hasn't signed a check in months."

"Oh, that's all taken care of by Juan Woodstock. His signature has been good here for years."

"How . . .? Does he have a power of attorney or something?"

"No, that has not been necessary. Your father and Juan

have been in here many times together discussing the movement of money between CDs and checking account or mutual funds or treasury notes. Juan Woodstock's signature is as good as Franklin Woodstock's."

He had not thought about it before. In fact, it was hard to imagine Johnny, about thirty years old, handling all the business transactions. It was a kind of shock to know that the young man was still using the surname of Woodstock, though he had used it all the way through public school.

"We cooperate in every way," the banker said. "It's the same as a joint account. As you know, your father's uncle was one of the founders of this institution. We give Juan every assistance we can. See that he has responsible help with income tax and such."

"Then you don't know whether Papa had two dollars in his pocket or a thousand? I guess that's what I wanted to know." He stood up.

"We cannot even guess. He often had cash. If you want records of the accounts, just let us know. Any time. If there's anything we can do, Mr. Woodstock."

Out on the street he started to walk around to his car, but saw in the courthouse parking area what well might be the Sheriff's car; at least it said on the side "Alamo County Sheriff's Dept." He jaywalked over to the grounds of the brown stone building which was the center of town.

It was a two-story Victorian-Gothic structure with a clock tower, an ambitious attempt to look as imposing as county courthouses farther east. There was a long-time joke that the clock was usually ten minutes off; people who were late always said that they went by the town clock. The evergreen trees and shrubs on the spacious lawn, plants which did not belong here, were another attempt to imitate civilization farther east.

The halls in the courthouse were floored with small white six-sided tiles. Brass spittoons decorated the floor at convenient intervals. The place always had a smell of the janitor's disinfectant. George's hand went unconsciously to his shirt collar, and he resented a feeling that he should be wearing a necktie.

Any idea of a need for formality disappeared in the sheriff's office. Sheriff Reynolds took his shiny boots off of his desk, stood up, shook hands, and called him "George." The sheriff was a lanky man with gray hair who looked as if he would be at home on a horse.

After some preliminary talk, the sheriff said, "Here's the way I see it: The old man either walked away from here, or he rode away from here, or he's still here. Now, we don't want to look like a bunch of fools. Is he still here?"

"What do you mean?"

"I mean could Clara Bender know where he's at, or Ed, or Miss Isabel out at the ranch, or anybody? Is there any way he could still be around here?"

"No, I don't think so, Sheriff."

"Well, he's been kind of cranky, you know. Old folks get that way. I thought maybe he got set against the nursing home and talked somebody into helping him hide out."

"I don't think so. Do you have a missing person bulletin, or whatever you call it, out on him?"

"Sure."

"Does that mean they're hunting him all over this part of the country?"

"No. No way you can do that. I've got a dozen missing person notices on file over there in the cabinet, and what it means is if we find a person or a body and don't know where it belongs, we go through the missing persons to check. That's all a sheriff or the police can do."

"Well, listen, Sheriff, I don't want to tell you your job,

but maybe we could have some search out in the country? I mean besides on Woodstock land. I believe Johnny is going over the ranch. . . ."

"He's got two hands helping, Buck and Slim. And that funny boy, Homer, for what he's worth."

"Good. What I was wondering was if we could get some search in every direction as far as a man could walk. Then maybe question everybody on the highways out of town that might have seen him. I don't know how you handle these things, but I imagine you have to stick to a budget. If there is any extra help needed or overtime, we would want to take care of it."

The sheriff nodded. "I got two deputies out on the town right now. If it turns out I need some money, I'll call Johnny."

"Good. We all appreciate your work on this thing."

CHAPTER TWO

Goodhaven

OUTSIDE on the street again, he began to harden his resolve about getting some facts out of the people at the nursing home. Ed had said that the nurses were impossible. He drove the Pontiac down a side street four blocks to the Goodhaven Nursing Home. The institution sat on a full city block, shaded by one grand old spreading live oak and a dozen smaller post oaks. Its patients, or clients, came from some distance, even from larger towns, for Goodhaven advertised that it provided easygoing country living.

Inside the front door he walked past the first offices and down to an area where the building seemed to branch into several halls. The whole place looked both cheap and sanitary. The nurse at the desk was writing on a chart at the same time that she talked and listened on the phone and smoked a cigarette.

Down one hall he saw a nurse pushing a cart loaded with various boxes of pasteboard and plastic. He went to her. "Excuse me, Miss. Could you tell me how to find a nurse that takes care of Mr. Franklin Woodstock?"

"He's not on this hall," she said. "Isn't he the old man that ran off?"

"Well, did you know anything about him? Did anybody see him leave?"

"He wasn't on my hall. I think he ran off on the three-to-eleven shift or the eleven-to-six shift. That's all I know."

"Thank you."

The nurse at the desk was off the phone. He went back to her. "Ma'am, I need to get some information about a patient, Mr. Franklin Woodstock."

"You from the newspaper?"

"No. I'm his son, George Woodstock."

"You a brother of Johnny Woodstock that runs the old ranch out there?"

"Well . . . uh . . . he runs the ranch. We are concerned about my father. We are trying to find any clues about where he might be. Maybe a nurse who took care of him could give suggestions about what he had on his mind the last week or so."

"I'm trying to bring the charts up for the next shift," she said. "We chart different things on different days of the week. Some things we chart every day, like doctor's new orders, vital signs, stuff like that. Then on certain days we chart different things: appetite, cooperation, recreation, weight of feces and urine for some, attitude of patient, stuff like that. Now, sir, I would like to tell you what is charted again and again about Mr. Franklin Woodstock: Stubborn! Will not eat boiled and mashed carrots. Stubborn! Will not accept bath. Stubborn! Will not allow aides to assist in toilet. Stubborn! Tries to pinch aide or nurse. Stubborn! Will not lay as asked in bed. Stubborn! Pulls out feeding tube. Stubborn! Broke injection needle. Stubborn! Will not swallow boiled and mashed vegetables. Stubborn! Spits out pills." She looked at him as if he were guilty.

He paused to be sure that she was through with her indictment, then said, "What we hoped was to find some idea about where he went. Could I talk to the nurse who took care of him?"

"Sally Medford is over there in the Medications Room. She's charge nurse on hall three, where he was at. She's busy. Don't say I sent you."

He went over to the door indicated. He could hear a mumbled conversation and decided not to knock. Inside two women dressed in white were seated at a table, bending over rows of bottles and trays of colored pills. "Miz Medford? Miz Sally Medford?"

The heavy-set woman who was pushing pills around in a tray with a small piece of cardboard stopped and stood up, her hands on hips. "You've made me lose count! What are you doing in here?"

He no sooner began to identify himself than she interrupted.

"Mister, can't you see that we are counting narcotics? In case you don't know, we have to justify every speck of narcotics at every shift change. I'm supposed to go home in fourteen minutes, and they will not okay one speck of overtime. What are you doing here? We have instructions to be friendly and helpful to family. Are you family?"

He told her again that he was George Woodstock and only wanted to know anything, any clues, as to what his father had been thinking in recent days. She seemed to understand about half of what he said.

She thrust one hand toward him. "See that thumb? That knuckle! That's where a patient bit me. Just bit me on purpose!"

"I'm sorry. Did Mr. Franklin Woodstock do that? How could it happen?"

"An old woman did it. I was cleaning her mouth. She's only got about seven teeth and she sunk every one into my thumb."

"Well, what we were thinking, Miz Medford, is that you might know what my father had on his mind lately. What he was thinking about."

"Mister, I've got eight feeders out there on hall three, four tube feeders, besides two colostomies and two on oxygen. And only two aides for twenty-nine patients in all. You think I have time to know what they have on their mind?"

"What was his attitude? Would you say he was stubborn?"

"Stubborn? For a man given only six months to live,

I would say he was stubborn. That was eight months ago. He would not lay like you turned him. If you don't turn these people they get decubitus. You know what decubitus is? Bed sores! The aides turn him, and quick as they leave the room he flops back over or gets up and sits in the chair."

"Did a doctor say he had six months to live?"

"Somebody said that's what they heard. I don't know if a doctor said it, but it's been eight months."

"Did he have bed sores?"

"Who knows? He didn't want anybody to touch his body. One time I asked him to go to the bathroom in a bedpan so we could weigh his output of feces and urine. You know what he said? 'Just put down forty pounds.' Another time he spit tobacco juice in a bedpan and told me to weigh it. He thought it was funny. You couldn't keep a roommate in the room with him. One roommate he had got just as stubborn as Mr. Woodstock was, and then he laughed so much he made himself sick at the stomach."

"Well, Miz Medford, I thought maybe you could give some kind of suggestion about what he had on his mind and where he might have gone."

"Maybe he went someplace where he could get food to suit him. He would eat in the dining room sometimes and eat everything in sight; then he might take it into his head not to eat for two days. And if you put a nose tube down and tried to feed him a liquid, he'd pull it out. That's all I know, Mister. It's past quitting time and we still haven't finished counting narcotics."

"When you are finished, would you be willing to stay a few minutes and answer a few more questions?"

"I can't. I've got two kids coming home from school, and when I'm not there they tear the place to pieces." She began to pay attention to the bottles and trays of pills.

"Well, thank you very much." He hoped he did not

sound as sarcastic as he felt. Heading back toward the front of the building, he renewed his determination to find someone who was willing and able to give out some reliable information.

The neat sign beside one open door read "Director of Nursing." In the small anteroom a young woman informed him: "Miss Teague is in conference with the administrator and the house doctor and others, Mr. Woodstock. If you'll wait, it shouldn't be over thirty minutes more. Just wait over in the Rec Room down there, and I'll call you."

He found the room she meant, a large space with tall windows across one wall, looking out on the lawn and oak trees. Before the windows a number of couches and stuffed chairs were drawn up, in them some dozen old people staring outside at the sunlit grounds. In one corner stood an upright piano, surrounded by a half-dozen patients, looking as if they expected the instrument to begin playing music. In another corner, on couches facing each other, sat a few old men and women talking to each other. Here and there scattered patients sat alone in wheelchairs or sturdy wooden chairs with arms.

Some of the old people had on ordinary street clothes. Some wore housecoats over pajamas or gowns. Several were bound to their chairs by broad straps. He did not count, but more than half were women, maybe twenty or thirty in all. They were of every size and shape, white-haired, wrinkled, some heavy, some so slight that they might not weigh seventy pounds. One old man was mumbling to himself. Most of them seemed to be staring at nothing.

George Woodstock, as he stood waiting, got a sudden question and a sudden revelation in his thoughts. What were they all staring at? What was in their minds? They were remembering their childhoods, their youths, their victories and defeats, many complicated lives, events, hopes, plans. One old woman was nodding as she sat, another, a gaunt figure with dark eyes, shook her head slowly as if saying "no" to everything.

Maybe some were thinking of a determination in middle age that they would accomplish something, like build a job shop machine shop system better than anything done before, one that would be a pattern for the future. He quickly rejected the thought and tried to see what those in front of the window were seeing. Out there in each tree hung one or two red plastic bird houses; sparrows or wrens flitted among the branches, singing, scolding, asserting themselves. Perhaps it was entertaining to those old ones who watched. One old man kept pointing, though no one paid much attention, to a red squirrel that moved quickly in the tailored forest.

George was thinking about finding a place to sit down when a well-dressed man about his own age entered and approached him.

"A nurse said you might be Mr. George Woodstock, the son of a patient here."

"I am. I'm just waiting."

The man shook hands and introduced himself as Douglas Albright from the oral history project at the university in Austin. They were eager to record a long interview with Mr. Franklin Woodstock whenever he became available. The man was aware that the old man was missing and just wanted to be brought up to date.

"We're searching, Mr. Albright," George said. "That's about all I can tell you."

"Please don't call me Mr. Albright or Dr. Albright. I hardly know who you mean. Everybody calls me 'Hap.' When I can get one of my elderly victims to call me 'Hap,' half the battle is won. They come to like me, and I come to like them. Man or woman."

"OK, Hap. But you'll have to call me 'George.'"

"I'll do it, George. If you have a few minutes, I'd like to

take the opportunity to assure you that the interview will actually be a pleasure to your father when he returns. Would you say that he is lucid, rather well in command of his faculties?"

"I don't know. He was sharp as ever when I saw him a year ago, but they say he did some funny things since then."

"You know, George, an old person will not remember last week, but may tell vivid details of seventy years ago. When anybody gets past ninety, we feel lucky to get some taped interview; but there is further reason to talk to Franklin Woodstock. I believe his father, Daniel Woodstock, was a mustanger in West Texas in the 1870s. And the boy, Franklin, maybe sixteen or eighteen, went to Wyoming or Utah to hunt wild horses one summer, though one doubts that there was much money in it so late. Did you know your grandfather, Daniel Woodstock?"

"Some," George said. "When I was little, he had a bad leg from riding broncs, and he lived in Decatur. Great-uncle Albert ran the ranch for Grandpaw. He used to drive to Decatur in our Model-T to see Grandpaw. Us kids thought he was great. Of course, I was too young to understand much about the mustanging business away back in the 1870s."

Hap Albright said, "They had their headquarters and corrals in Grayson County and went out west as far as the Caprock. At a time when the Apaches and Comanches and Kiowas were still giving trouble."

George remembered some detail. "Papa said they broke the likely ones to the saddle and the swayback nags to harness for the farmers in East Texas. The real mean ones, they couldn't stand to shoot, so they turned them loose. That's Grandpaw and his bunch. I don't know what Papa did with any horses he caught. I guess he just admired the old man so much that he tried to do the same thing, about forty years too late."

The efficient office girl was calling his name. "It will be up to Papa, Hap, when we find him."

"Okay. Thanks, George."

In the office of the Director of Nursing, he seated himself with a confused determination to get some facts. Miss Teague was a dignified woman with dyed brown hair piled high on her head.

"Mr. Woodstock, we have talked several times, on the phone and face to face, with Mr. Juan Woodstock and Ms. Clara Bender, both of whom, I understand, are related to our patient. And I believe that it is time to speak with perfect candor about the general situation, about what a nursing home can do and what it cannot do, what it is for and what it is not for."

George did not see any point in trying to explain that Juan Woodstock was not related to Papa. "Excuse me," he said. "Was your conference just now about my father? What was decided?"

"I'm glad you asked that, Mr. Woodstock. It gives me just the correct opportunity to explain. Your father was mentioned along with a dozen other problems. We have nearly 200 patients here. Every family tends to think that we have only their father or mother or uncle or aunt. That is natural. I understand. Family members must understand too.

"Mr. Woodstock, a family does not wish to care for an older person who may require much attention. An old person, however much loved, may be contrary, stubborn, requiring constant attention. So they pass the job to a nursing home. They are too busy, have their own lives to live. They tell themselves that they don't understand medicine; therefore, they do not need to take care of the old mother or father. That is the easy way out. That is about the only way out. But a family member cannot expect the kind of care in a nursing home which he wishes he had time to give at home to the patient.

"Mr. Woodstock, we have all kinds of people here. A few decades ago we had insane asylums, such as those at Wichita Falls and Terrell and Austin; an ambulatory elder person who acted peculiar was sent to such a place. Today those same persons are put in nursing homes and are supposed to be controlled and kept happy with a careful selection of drugs. They . . ."

"Excuse me, Ma'am. Are you saying that Franklin Woodstock was crazy?"

"No, I am not. I am trying to give an idea of the variety of patients in this institution and the difficulty of satisfying family members. Last week we had two complaints about old people being restrained, one in bed, one in a jury chair. They were horrified at mother or daddy being tied up. Then on Sunday an old lady fell out of her wheelchair and broke her hip, and her daughter demanded to know why she had not been tied in so she could not fall.

"Mr. Woodstock, a month or so ago we had a bad case of staph infection. It's highly contagious. It took three days to get the patient transferred to a hospital. Our aides do not know, and are not supposed to know, the proper procedures for sterile handling of laundry, their own persons and such. During those three days, I and the senior nurse here worked around the clock caring for that old man and making certain that the infection did not spread.

"People do not understand, Mr. Woodstock, what the cost would be to care for an elderly patient around the clock with the personal attention which they expect. We pay LVNs about six to seven dollars an hour, RNs a bit more; aides, who are unskilled, we pay the minimum wage. It would take three nurses for a patient to go around the clock, and that means seven days a week, besides more overtime to overlap shifts. Consider that cost. Plus medications. Plus daily doctor's visits. Plus special foods and special preparation. Plus laundry. Plus maintenance and utilities. Plus. . . ."

"Excuse me! I understand, Miss Teague." The lecture had become irritating. "I only wanted to ask a few questions. Is it your guess that the nurses here—they feel antagonistic about the patients?"

She stared at him a moment. "I am glad you asked that question. It will help you understand. A young aide or even a trained nurse takes care of a patient for months, tries to ease his pain, as if he were a baby. And what's the end of it? He dies. The aide goes home and cries about it. We average nearly two deaths a month in this institution. I tell the nurses not to cry. It's not professional. But they find it difficult to be cheerful and optimistic and loving one week, then not care the following week. Have you ever taken care of a person for a week or more while they die?"

"I understand, Miss Teague. What I was hoping was to get some more specific information about Franklin Woodstock."

She said, "I was coming to that. In regard to an antagonistic attitude which you ask about. A good competent, mature nurse was required to resign a few months ago because of her treatment of your father. He was not eating well, and we found that this nurse was bringing in food from her home to give to him. Apparently she was broiling steak and grinding it up in a food chopper and mixing it with mushroom soup, then keeping it hot for him in a thermos dish. That is not all. She was also bringing him a thermos bottle of cold beer. She sat right there where you sit and wept when I told her we must have her resignation. It had been suggested that Franklin Woodstock was paying her to bring in food, but I thought it beside the point and did not even ask her. My point is this: Where does this example leave your suggestion that a nurse may be antagonistic toward a patient?"

"I don't see why she was fired myself."

"She was released because we have a full-time nutrition expert here. We have doctors' orders about various diets. We have menus planned and approved well in advance. We have a state board which sends inspection teams here, sometimes on schedule, sometimes on surprise visits, and they examine everything that goes on. That is why she was required to resign."

"Could I talk to that nurse? Does she live around here?"

"No. I understand that she moved to Denver or somewhere back in February."

He stood up. "Well, thank you for your time, Miss Teague." He had come to understand Ed Bender's statement that the people at the nursing home were impossible.

Out in the parking lot he briefly wished that his older brother Walter, the take-charge Harvard man, were there. See how they acted to a man who was as evasive and inclined to lecture as they were. Walter and Miss Teague would be a good match; they deserved each other.

It had not been clear a year or so ago just what a nursing home meant. Walter, along with a local doctor, had made the decision to put Papa in a home where he could get regular medications and the best professional care. Evidently Papa himself had not realized what it meant either.

Sitting with his hands on the steering wheel in the parking lot, George thought of one more visit, to the newspaper, the bi-weekly *Banner.* Maybe some of the townspeople would come up with some clues. But it was clear that the news was already all over town, and if anybody knew anything and were willing to tell it, they would do it. Also, he didn't even know what day the paper came out, and Johnny might already have more news.

He had not eaten since a doughnut and a cup of coffee at five-thirty that morning. Izzy would give him some supper or a snack or something. It was with a curious flood of relief that he turned the Pontiac out toward the ranch, as if he turned his back on a hectic world and his face toward a simple, straightforward life he had once known long ago.

CHAPTER THREE

The Ranch

THE northwest corner of Woodstock land just touched the city limits of the town. It was a ranch of moderate size for that region, larger than most but much smaller than the few largest spreads of the South Plains. It covered twelve sections, or square miles, something over seven thousand acres. Here Franklin Woodstock had reared his sons and daughters with certain strict, old-fashioned methods, had built up the ranch with hard work and shrewd management, had seen his wife die in middle age, and had grown old. The children, grandchildren, great-grandchildren, and great-great-grandchildren were now scattered from New York to San Francisco, from Atlanta to Denver and Tucson.

George passed by the turn-off at the well-graded county road and went on a half mile to the old wagonroad, knowing as he did it that he had succumbed briefly to that old nostalgia. Along this winding road he had ridden horseback to school with Walter, Clara, Clarence, and Irma more than a half century ago. Even some of the trees he knew individually, for some mesquites seem to live forever, growing slowly, accenting their gnarled and stunted twistings. He knew a certain chaparral thicket which had always grown thick and secret cover for cottontails. He knew a prickly pear thicket always piled in the middle with cow chips and horse apples and dead gray bits of wood gathered by rats, where they raised their young, depending on the thorns of the leafy cactus to keep the coyotes out. He knew a swale of low ground where evening primroses always bloomed; they flowered this late, but were closed up now from the sun, waiting for the evening. He drove through the prairie dog town, four or five acres nearly bare of grass, dotted with reddish clay mounds; a half dozen of the little creatures sat erect and perfectly still beside their holes. He remembered Papa's repeated warning that when they got to eating as much grass as the cows, he would declare war on them; but as if they knew the warning, they had accepted a truce, and their claim of land had remained the same size.

It did not seem remarkable to him that the road led around to the side and rear of the large Victorian-era ranch house; seldom if ever anyone had come to the front door. The white paint was peeling on the house, but it still looked imposing in front of the smokehouse, a long metal implement shed, two unpainted barns, the lots, chicken houses, and two windmills.

Around the house a woven-wire fence protected Izzy's flower-beds from grazing livestock. There was never enough water for a lawn, so she made little raised plots of good soil for flowers; some of them were shaped and contained by worn tractor tires lying on the dry soil.

Two pickups were parked around back, and a saddled horse was tied to the yard gatepost. Before he got the gate open, Izzy came running out the kitchen door to hug him. "George. George," she said. "I prayed you'd come."

A big black dog, Gabe, came out from under the smokehouse to be petted, wagging his tail. He was old, but not old enough to remember George. The hug from Izzy had told Gabe that here was someone who belonged.

Izzy's face showed delight at seeing him, also worry. She undoubtedly had been crying. A short woman with bright brown eyes, she had always tried to mother them, though she was probably no older than George. "I meant to ride out and catch them," she said. "And help search. Soon as I took the bread out of the oven. They didn't eat since breakfast. They went out to Plum Creek, towards the big east tank."

He immediately offered to take the horse in her place, and she agreed. When he mounted she said, *"Por favor* . . . watch Homer."

He assured her that he would, then lined the long-legged bay out east in an easy lope. Though not an avid fan of riding, he found it a relief to actually be doing something, taking action which might be of some help. The vision of the old man, lying sick and helpless in a gully, returned. The bay gelding understood that he was supposed to catch up with the riders ahead, and he needed no guidance; he turned right or left to avoid a patch of mesquite or a clump of chaparral.

In little more than a mile George saw them stopped ahead. Johnny was trying to help Homer remount his horse, and the two hands were watching, laughing. It was a patient old horse called "Baldy," probably twenty years old, known to have a jolting trotting gait. It was not the horse's fault that Homer had fallen off.

As George rode up, Johnny pushed Homer into the saddle, but the clumsy, overgrown kid never got his balance; he fell off on the right hand side, clawing leather. The two hands, Slim and Buck, thought it hilarious. Patient Johnny and the patient horse tried again, this time successfully.

"Keep both hands on the saddle horn," Johnny said. He tied the reins together over old Baldy's neck. "Leave the reins alone."

There was no question as to who was in charge of the search. Johnny. The young Chicano could give direct orders without being bossy. He said to the two hands, who had quit laughing when George rode up, "Slim, you go on across the creek and comb downstream a couple of hundred yards wide. Buck, you do the same on this side. I'll try to stay right in the creek bed as much as I can; there's not much water. We ought to make it to the north fence line by dark. George, uh. . . ."

George understood the situation and said, "I'll ride with Homer, and we'll search on this side."

Homer had not said a word during the process of remounting old Baldy, had only grunted a little. The youngster, nearly as big as a man, had a heavy look about his body and movements. George reined the bay over near enough to pat the old horse on the neck, then moved ahead in a walk. Old Baldy understood; he followed. Homer hunkered down over the saddle horn and squinted toward Johnny and the two cowhands as they went forward searching.

Slim and Buck were halfway tenant farmers. Each of them lived on a 320-acre tract of Woodstock land with sixty acres under cultivation. They paid as rent one-third of their crop and got free grazing for saddle horses and a mule team and a milk cow and a couple of beeves to butcher. It was a system worked out by old Franklin Woodstock; he had a bunkhouse, and earlier he had hired men as he needed them, but found himself hiring inexperienced kids and broken-down grocery clerks. Now he always had at least two top cowhands on call; together with Johnny, who could do the work of about two hands, they had been able to work the ranch. Slim and Buck did not complain about the sorry wages; when they worked for the old man, they got thirty dollars for a hard ten-hour day. In addition to their large family gardens, they produced hay and maize crops, cow feed, on their sixty-acre plots; they always found a ready market, at top prices, from their landlord for every bundle or bale of their two-thirds of the crop.

George could see at times the Chicano rider through the leaves of hackberry, willow, and oak. The little stream was intermittent, nothing but damp sand and gravel in places, knee deep to a horse in other places. Every half mile or less a crossing was cut out, worn undoubtedly by the sharp hooves of buffalo and deer for hundreds of years, now kept clear by Hereford cattle. The three searchers were doing an efficient job.

Homer did as well as he could. He squinted and looked to the right and left as he hunkered over the saddle horn. He had a peculiar habit of slapping a hand over one eye and peering intently with the other, as if one eye or the other were giving him a mistaken picture of the world. George felt that he was doing his share of the work by merely looking after the clumsy youth.

As the sun touched the western horizon they came to the north fence line, and Johnny waved them back. It was dark by the time they unsaddled in the harness shack and gave each mount a quart of oats. The old man had an iron-clad rule that every horse worked had to be fed grain.

Izzy searched their faces a moment and did not ask whether they had found anything. Slim and Buck had planned to drive straight home to their own families, but when they smelled the fresh yeast bread she had baked they decided to stay for supper. There was a beef roast and creamed potatoes and English peas fresh from the garden and peach cobbler from fruit canned a year ago.

Pushing his chair in, George said that it had been a long day, and since there were still mattresses on some of the cots in the bunkhouse, he would sleep there.

"No," Izzy ordered, "Go to your old room. I change the fresh sheets every month even if no one comes to sleep. There are clean towels in the south bathroom." She was smiling to hide a little wave of pain in her face.

He could have walked to the room and inside it with his eyes closed. It was full of memories. Of a time when there had been no bathrooms. When he and Walter and Clarence had shared the place and had been required to wash their bare feet on the back gallery before going to bed. Now he could almost hear out there by the big fireplace Papa's booming voice, slightly nasal, often accompanied by laughter. Surely it could not be that the voice was now somewhere weak or whining or still.

In the morning George's sister Clara came in before breakfast. She was a blowzy, generously built woman who dyed her gray hair reddish blond and curled it. She showed her age more than the others of her generation, but seemed to have plenty of energy. Now she went about the house chattering to everyone and pretended to help Izzy set the table. "George," she said, "you must not start home until Pauline brings little Annie. I told her to come this morning."

But her daughter-in-law, who came after the early breakfast, did not bring the child. Clara was full of questions. "Pauline, why didn't you bring Annie? Where is Annie? I asked you to bring Annie."

"Annie is in school where she belongs," the younger woman said. Clara raised her eyebrows in an exaggerated manner. "Well, I should think she could afford to miss one day of school to see her own grandmother and her great-uncle George."

It was obvious that Pauline did not take her mother-in-law too seriously. "I sent Annie to school for punishment. The little snip! She disobeyed me."

As if trying to avert a quarrel, Izzy said, "Let me cook you some scrambled eggs and sausage, Pauline honey. The biscuits are still hot."

"Thanks, Izzy. I've eaten. I was out of the house only an hour or so last evening, and what does Annie do? She gets into my clothes closet and puts on my best dress and gets into my lipstick and puts on my high-heel shoes.

Then Miss Annie parades herself in front to the mirror."

Clara said, "How could an eight-year-old girl hurt your best dress?"

"Dragging the hem all around on the floor, that's how."

George also thought it a good idea to stop the argument. He took Clara by the arm, asked if he could talk to her a minute, and drew her into the hall. She said, Yes, that she had called Walter in New York; then later she had called Clarence and Irma.

"What did Walter say?"

"Well, you know Walter. He said to get you out here and get information from the nursing home and get the sheriff working on it and have Johnny search the ranch good."

"Is Walter coming?"

"He said he can't. He was put out with us. Like he said, Papa could not have vanished into thin air."

"Well, look, Sis, I have to go back. Johnny will search. I have business in the shop that won't wait. I'll call Walter."

At eight-thirty he called back home to the shop. Robert Fowler answered, Yes, that he would accept a collect call from George Woodstock. The new man said that everything was going okay, everyone was busy, but there were a couple of problems.

"What are the problems, Bob?"

"Well, they are not really problems. I just wanted to know your idea. I cut the form blocks out of scrap and have them about finished except for the radius around the top. There's a quarter radius and a three-sixteenth radius. Some big shops would buy new mill cutters and have a cutter grinder put the radius in them. But you know what they charge, and we might not need the cutters again for a long time. I have some fast cutting files and I can do it nearly as fast as on a mill."

"Did you put any spring-back on the blocks, Bob?"

"Well, it's half-hard aluminum parts, Mr. Woodstock. I put three degrees. In other words, eighty seven instead of ninety. If that's not enough spring-back when they go to run the parts on a hydraulic press, we would still have stock to take off and could save the form blocks."

"That all sounds good to me. What's the other problem? You said there are a couple."

"Well, yesterday afternoon two guys were in here with a job for us to bid. It's just pieces of angle iron machined on the outside and hole patterns in both legs. I would bid it low myself; it's only eighteen parts, but I got the idea they may want a bunch later. After we got the drill plates made, the hands you have here could do most of the work. If it turns out they want a hundred later, and we already had the tooling made, we could beat any other bids and still clean up. But I don't want to bid anything without your ideas. They want a price today."

"OK, Bob. I'll be in by noon or early this afternoon. We'll give them a price today."

He was elated when about nine-thirty he drove the Pontiac out the ranch road and nosed it east on the highway. The new man, Bob Fowler, seemed to know what he was doing, had initiative, was exactly the type needed for the great plan of the best, most profitable tooling shop in the country.

As he drove George alternated between several thoughts and emotions. If only Papa had transferred the hundred thousand to him before now. Or would turn up in good shape and mentally alert, laughing at them for their concern. George was ready for the investment now, not some day, ready to buy some more equipment, ready to hire some men and check them out. After all, he was no spring chicken himself.

But then he would feel guilty about such thoughts and would feel almost like a little boy searching for his father.

George W. Woodstock graduated from high school in

the spring of 1939. He had never been fond of schoolwork. Living so far from school made it hard to practice for sports, and there were no courses such as shopwork. Though Papa had been ready to send him away to college, he decided against it. He wanted to work with his hands, something practical.

He got a job as a rod man on a land surveying crew. From there he went to work as an instrument man on a surveying crew for the principal dirt contractor on a dam across Red River between Denison, Texas, and Durant, Oklahoma. There, on what was then the largest earth-fill dam in the world, he became crew chief and took responsibility on the graveyard shift for all grade stakes in the spillway excavation and dam slopes. When they would not pay him more than twenty-five dollars a week, he quit and went to work for the U.S. Corps of Engineers, which was then feverishly laying out new airfields and enlarging old ones in the anticipation of war. He worked as surveying instrument man on an airfield at Grand Junction, Colorado, and one at Greenville, Texas.

He had registered for the military draft and saw young men his own age being taken into the service. There had been a requirement for aviation cadet training that an applicant must have four years of college work. Then it had been reduced to two years. When, after Pearl Harbor, the requirement was reduced to a high school diploma, George took the cadet test at Dallas and passed it. He was sworn into the air corps of the army in the summer of 1942.

After classification as a navigator at Santa Ana, California, he went through classes at two different bases—classes in meteorology, Morse code, electricity, radio, military courtesy, dead reckoning, pilotage, map projections, optics. Then he went to the advanced navigation school at Hondo, Texas, where they regularly flew navigation missions over the forty-eight states, using celestial, radio, and dead reckoning. He was chewed out for some shortcoming at every army base, but graduated at the top of his class in his air-work grades. A young Swede from Wisconsin who had a degree in math, beat him out in ground classwork.

George's bombing crew went into the Pacific with the 7th Air Force, which flew for Admiral Nimitz. At Hickam Field he had a short course which was supposed to prepare navigators for long over-water flights. The instructor, a captain, had invented a new, complicated method of getting a fixed position from one sextant shot on the sun. George rebelled against it as impossible and kept from getting into serious trouble only by exerting all his will power to keep from calling a superior officer "stupid." He bought a book on spherical trig in Honolulu and a few months later would send back through channels a convincing debunking of the captain's idea; the captain would be removed from his post.

The crew went to Kwajalein first. They struck against Jaluit, Wake, and Truk. Then they moved to Guam, from which they struck against Yap, Marcus, Truk, Chichi Jima, Haha Jima, Iwo Jima. George became a flight navigator and a first lieutenant. He often marvelled that his crew and the crews who followed him seemed to trust so fully in his navigation, not knowing the difficulty from changing winds over these hundreds of miles of trackless water wilderness. Their missions, night and day, averaged ten or eleven hours long.

George had a certain bitterness about the decoration orders that came through, for distinguished flying crosses, air medals, oak leaf clusters, battle stars. They were automatic, and good men died on their twenty-fourth mission and, therefore, never got their DFC. He thought he had earned one medal: for the paper which had stopped the fool captain's false navigation system and may well have saved some lives. But the establishment, of course, was not going to admit that a stupid waste of time had been going on.

He was back in the States by the time the Bomb was dropped and the Japanese surrendered. The Air Corps would not let him go into navigation research, though he had worked in one of the difficult theaters of the war and had used Loran, a new navigation device. So he got his discharge.

He had been an assistant civil engineer for the Corps of Engineers at the time he swore in, and every veteran had his old job guaranteed to him. He went back to surveying for the government at $1,440 per year, working on a dam on the Brazos, later to be Lake Whitney. He dated and married Helen. They lived in trailer houses for several years while he went from job to job, wherever the Corps of Engineers sent him.

When she became pregnant, she demanded that they settle down. He reluctantly agreed. He got a job as a beginning machinist for Chance-Vought Aircraft between Dallas and Fort Worth.

Quickly he moved to the tooling department and realized that he had found his life's work. Helen had been right about settling down. The thing about tooling, it was all custom work; sometimes there was a tool design and sometimes not. Even if you had prints, they didn't tell you how to do it. You could use your own ideas and common sense. But Vought company policies and Union Local 893 would not let him progress as fast as his work deserved, so he quit and went to work for job shops in the area. Because of his experience as a surveyor and navigator, he was able to catch on quickly to the measuring and math problems.

Once, half drunk and feeling sentimental, he told Helen: "When I die, all I want on my tombstone is this: Surveyor, Navigator, Tool and Die Maker, Son of Franklin Woodstock."

CHAPTER FOUR

Walter

It took George about three hours at the shop to make sure everything was going all right and to confirm Robert Fowler's bid on the new work. He called in the bid and got the job immediately. He was highly pleased that the new man could handle whatever needed doing.

At home Helen said, "George, am I ever glad to see you. Your brother in New York has called half a dozen times trying to get you at the ranch and everywhere." She was inclined to exaggerate.

"What did Walter want now?"

"Why, he wanted to talk to you. Not Clara or Ed or Frederick or Johnny. You."

"I'll call him after a while. Is there any way a hungry, tired man could get a little supper around here?"

About six o'clock, aware that it was seven in New York, he got hold of Walter at his home. His elder brother asked, "What the hell is going on down there, George?"

"Well, if you talked to Clara and Ed and Johnny, you know as much about it as I do."

"What did the people at Goodhaven say?"

He recounted his actions and lack of success at the nursing home.

"You'll have to go to the top manager, George, and the owners."

"I thought the nurses that took care of Papa would know more about Papa's health and what he had in mind."

"They would, but you've got to put pressure on them

from up above to get their cooperation. George, I want you to take charge of this project and find Papa or his body. You're within a reasonable distance. I trust you more than Clara or Clarence or Irma. And you are there handy."

With some feeling of resentment George said, "Actually it's not all that handy, Walter."

"Don't you want to find Papa?"

"Look, dammit! I've just spent two days going out there to see what I could do. Don't sit up there in New York and tell me I don't care."

They talked five minutes without saying anything new. Several times Walter repeated the inane, "He could not have vanished into thin air." Finally Walter asked, "Can you pick me up at the airport Wednesday morning? And drive me out to Woodstock? I want to get to the bottom of this whole thing."

"All right. You call me at the shop or here at home when you get in. I can pick you up in thirty minutes." It meant another couple of days or more away from the shop, hauling his older brother around. But it could be that Walter, with his pushy ways, would find out things which he, George, had not been able to. Then, also, Walter was a take-charge type that is hard to say No to.

The eldest son had gone to Texas Technological College at Lubbock a year, then to Southern Methodist University to take a Bachelor's degree in business administration. The old man, trying to give each of his offspring the opportunity which suited him or her, had offered to send Walter to any school in the country. Walter had chosen the Harvard Business School, where he took a graduate degree with high honors. He had advanced up the ladder of success in corporate management ever since.

It was the middle of the morning when Walter called from the airport. George left immediately to pick him up. The man, at the age of sixty-nine, still managed to appear dapper. A young porter in uniform put the two bags in the back seat, and Walter gave him a one-dollar bill. He was one of those people who always knows exactly how much to tip; in fact, by his manner he established the amount of the tips for various services.

"You're still driving the old Pontiac," Walter said. "Must be a good automobile."

"I keep it in good shape. It's only got ninety thousand miles on it."

After they headed out the highway west, Walter said, "I'm glad we have a chance for a good talk. I know you were out here for a few days and it was inconvenient. I appreciate it. Clara, Clarence, and Irma certainly ought to appreciate it. We need someone we can count on. The estate is worth more than any of us realize, much more. I hope you know that I trust you and will back you up."

"The trouble is," George said, "I've got three hands working for me that need to be told what to do, and the closest I have to a lead man is a guy that's been working for me about a week. It's hard to make a go of a tooling shop like that."

"George, I know what you mean. For about four hours yesterday I sat in on negotiations, the results of which were that one corporation loaned another corporation seven million dollars. I don't want to sound like a big shot, but our company works mostly as management consultants now. That means that we are involved in detailed operations in a number of corporations, even to the extent of partial ownership. I could talk about the widow and orphan stockholders, but the fact is that thousands of solid citizens expect us to do our work, and many management personnel rely on our careful services. I am not free to fly down to Texas just anytime I want to. What I would like to do is look things over carefully out here, then you and I can communicate by phone, and we can see that the thing is done right."

George was thinking, *No, you don't want to sound like a big shot. Not you.* His brother's proposition, if that was what it was, did not seem to require an answer.

Three minutes down the highway, Walter started another assertion of opinion. "George, our biggest problem is Johnny. That situation bothers me."

"I was thinking," George said, "how lucky we are to have Johnny to run the ranch."

"Not that. That's not what I mean. If we had a clear contract with him it would be different. Let me draw a scenario. Out of nowhere this Mexican girl shows up at the ranch. She's pregnant. Izzy probably had to leave home because she got pregnant without a husband; you know how these Catholics are. Anyway, Papa felt sorry for her. In those days he was hiring hands as he needed them, and he couldn't get a decent cook to work part time and feed a crew of hungry men. So he gave Izzy a chance, and she learned to cook."

George interrupted. "You don't think Johnny was born yet when she came."

"My best guess is that he was born four or five months after she moved in."

"Why would Papa hire a pregnant woman for heavy cooking duties?"

"Look, George, this is my version. I don't know the details, but this is undoubtedly what happened. She probably cried when she asked for a job. Papa was a sucker for a crying female."

"Well, Walt, I guess Clara was the only kid around Woodstock when Izzy came, and she was busy with her own kids. I know once she acted like there was a secret to it when Irma was there. I guess the idea of Izzy having an illegitimate kid was too sinful for Irma to hear about."

"Clara is a dingbat, George."

They drove in silence for a couple of minutes, then Walter went on. "The point is that they have moved in.

Izzy and Johnny are the only people that regularly live at ranch headquarters, unless that idiot kid Homer is out there. They run the place. They decide what has to be decided. They have moved in. It's not a good situation."

George ventured, "We could not get a better ranch manager than Johnny."

"For chasing cows, yes. For digging post holes. George, I don't have any prejudice against minority people. But this property, which Papa earned by the sweat of his brow over many years, is more valuable than any of us realize. What does Johnny know about the efficient management of a big enterprise? I guess he finished high school. He can calculate so many pounds of beef at so many cents per pound. But how about a computer system that integrates the activities of a large enterprise? Johnny would be lost. But there he is. He moved in."

The crack about finishing high school did not set well with George. He said, "You seem to take it for granted that Papa is dead."

"No, not at all. We have to get some of these people on the ball, and let's find him. What I do assume is this: Papa is ninety-one years old. We have to find him and see that he is well cared for. But the fact is, he is as good as dead in so far as managing his affairs. He is *non compos mentis,* as the legal boys say."

In the town of Woodstock, George agreed to haul Walter around but refused to go into the interviews with him. Walter came out of the Goodhaven Nursing Home after two hours. He was angry.

Walter said, slamming the car door harder than necessary, "The people who have the final authority make themselves unavailable. We'll see about that! At least I got some phone numbers. They're going to find out that I have contacts all over this country. Three or four of the personnel in that nursing home are going to lose their jobs. One thing I cannot stand is inefficiency."

The older brother seemed to have better cooperation at the sheriff's office; at least he did not threaten to have anyone fired. But after a session at the bank he came out frowning and shaking his head. He said, "George, these small-town bankers are fifty years behind the times. They are too casual. It's ridiculous. Those old days of a handshake and a general understanding are past. They have got hundreds of verbal agreements and understandings in that place. I see one thing. We're going to have to get some good accountants in here to find out exactly what's going on."

They went out to the ranch. When Walter had got one bag out, he said, "Aren't you going to lock your car?"

George laughed. "Nope."

Izzy came out the back door, and Walter was subjected to a hugging whether he wanted it or not. Johnny was out with Homer and the two hands searching to the southeast past the old homestead place and out around Dead Cowbones Bluff. When Izzy discovered they had not eaten dinner, she insisted on cooking them a fast supper.

The searchers did not come in until nearly midnight, worn out, having found nothing. George got to bed quickly. His older brother took half an hour to shower and put on his pajamas. More like an old maid than a boy raised on a ranch, George thought.

In the middle of the morning Walter put a reward notice in the bi-weekly *Banner:* "One thousand dollars for information leading to the discovery of the whereabouts of Franklin Woodstock." He had apparently gathered all the information he wanted for the time being. They headed east in the Pontiac.

"George, let's take this time to go over a few matters of importance. Papa is somewhere, dead or alive. I have connections with a detective agency in St. Louis. They occasionally do some indispensable work for us finding information that would not otherwise be available. They are very competent and very discreet, will go anywhere in the country. I'm going to have them put a man on this job, some fellow who will dig into it and persist until he gets answers. As of now the situation is impossible. When the detective comes down here I'm going to insist that all the kin cooperate with him one hundred percent.

"Then I'm going to send an accountant down here with a letter of introduction that authorizes him to inspect every transaction that went through the bank relating to the ranch, income taxes and everything, for the past thirty years.

"Which brings up the problem of Johnny. You know, George, the boy cannot manage a large enterprise. There are fantastic possibilities in Papa's holdings. You know, there are hundreds of high-class people in the cities who would like a piece of land they could call a ranch, if it were convenient to them and presented right. I'm talking about men who are accustomed to hearing the price of land quoted by the square foot. A piece of land needed by a developer may go for thirty-five or fifty dollars a square foot. And many a small house lot, a quarter acre, sells for twenty to fifty thousand dollars.

"Twelve sections is seven thousand, six-hundred and eighty acres. Suppose you divided five thousand of that into ten-acre plots and sold each one for fifty thousand. That's only five thousand an acre. That's twenty-five million right there. Now, there's no way you can do that unless you know what you're doing. You have to build a helicopter pad and a landing strip for light aircraft. You must make it exclusive. No low-class people."

"You mean no blacks or Jews?"

"No, George, I mean no anybody unless they want a peaceful retreat that's both rustic and has the conveniences they are accustomed to. You could have a restriction that a trailer house could not be parked on one of the ranches more than two weeks. The owners would be required to build substantial houses."

"Then you mean rich people."

"I mean people who can afford it. The idea of being exclusive is a selling point, like membership in a country club. You build a golf course and a big lake on Plum Creek. You keep it stocked with fish. You keep two thousand, six hundred and eighty acres unsold and raise quail and dove for hunting. I'll tell you something that would add to the appeal. That damned red-clay flat below Dead Cowbones Bluff—that's where those bone scientists, paleontologists, found dinosaur bones. A lot of high-class people would be thrilled to think they are so far out in the country that you can find dinosaur bones and Indian arrowheads. As long as everything was convenient."

George asked, "Where does all this money come from to build a golf course and a landing strip and a big lake?"

"No problem. If you have a plan and twelve sections of land with a clear title, you can get all the financing you need. I think I'm as good an authority on borrowing money as you can find in the country. No problem at all. You have to invest money to make money."

George was troubled by the proposition. He said, "It seems like the way we're talking, we have given up on Papa. Like he's gone. And I think Clara and Clarence and Irma will want to have their say."

Walter insisted, "I have not given up on Papa. I tell you I will have a detective on it within one week. As for Irma and Clarence and Clara, I hope you will help me to show them the sanity of our position. If we only get one to go along, we can outvote the other two. If we find Papa alive, we have all the evidence and reason we need to have a guardian appointed by a court to take care of him and his assets. I assure you of that.

"I mentioned the sale of land in small blocks to the

tune of twenty-five million. That's only the beginning. We form a construction company to build custom ranch-style houses. We form a company to drill water wells. There is underground water all over the land. We have the inside track to sell anything from fish bait to motorboats. We could have a riding stables.

"I believe a court would quickly appoint a guardian from Papa's own children. Especially someone who had management experience."

George was thinking, *I wonder who you have in mind, you son-of-a-bitch.* He felt repugnance toward Walter's entire scheme and could not help wondering whether it was a selfish thought on his part. If the place was tied up in a land deal or if Walter was appointed guardian, he certainly would not get the hundred thousand bucks for his shop any time soon.

Walter went on. "Some of Papa's descendants need money very much more than I do, George. Papa and I were very much alike. He built that place from nothing. He had initiative and big ideas. I don't want to sound like a big shot, but if you have big ideas, and understand management, there is no end to what may be accomplished. I am willing to put my training and experience to work for the five direct heirs. I'll need the assistance of my brothers and sisters who are closer to the action and perhaps are not so busy as I am."

It was a relief to dump the older brother at the taxi zone in front of the American Airlines terminal, without even knowing the next departure time north. The last George saw of him Walter was summoning a "boy" to carry his bags.

The drive back had taken less than three hours, but it had seemed like ten.

CHAPTER FIVE

Private Investigator

THE work at the shop was piling up, and George was thinking about asking the men to work overtime during the weekend. Some calculations showed that he could pay time-and-a-half on a couple of jobs and still come out okay. Then a seedy-looking old man named Wiggins presented himself, looking for work.

George asked the man, "Are you a tool and die maker?"

"I've had experience," Wiggins said. "I'd like to see the foreman or the owner."

George had on a greasy shop apron. "I'm the owner. Are you a tool and die maker?"

The man had on a baggy suit which looked as if it had been slept in for two weeks, but George had made it a rule that you cannot always judge a hand by appearances. Wiggins was from Detroit and said that he had worked around a number of shops. He claimed that he could do good B-class work, but would have to get eighteen dollars an hour.

George did some quick mental calculation about the cost of working the other hands overtime. "I'm willing to give you a tryout, but the pay is eight dollars an hour."

"They don't pay much around here, do they? Could you make it ten?"

"Nope."

"I'll take it, but I wouldn't want to do much close work for that kind of money. Then I'll need a fifty dollar advance on my wages to tide me over a few days."

George had that amount in his wallet, but felt a little suspicious and wanted a witness. He got Bob Fowler into the small office and introduced the two. Then he paid the advance. "Bob is a sort of lead man. Either him or me will give you your jobs and help you get started. When can you start? When can you bring in your tool boxes?"

"I can start right now. But my tools are up in Detroit. I'll have to get them shipped down here. I thought I could use some of yours like you've got in those boxes there or the other guys' tools."

That stopped George for a minute. Then he said, "We'll try to furnish tools a few days while we see if we can use you. Come in tomorrow morning at eight o'clock."

After the old man left, Bob Fowler chuckled and said, "Reckon you hired a wino?"

"I don't know. Let's give him a chance. Say, Bob, we can take my little metal box out there for him. Watch him when he uses my tools, will you? I don't want him hammering with my mikes."

Only three days after he came back from Woodstock, George got a long-distance call in the evening from W. H. Dobbs, a private investigator. He said that Mr. Walter Woodstock had assured him that he would get complete cooperation from all the family members of the missing man. George assured him that he would.

Dobbs had a kind of raspy voice. He said, "I'd like to call on you about a week from now, sometime when you have a few hours to discuss the issues. And I'd like to ask you to prepare yourself to go into the possibilities in depth."

George said, "I mean to help any way I can."

"Well, Mr. Woodstock, people are often reluctant to be candid about members of their own family. Certainly I shall work with the police or other officer of the law. I may find it necessary to go to New Mexico on a lead, or to East Texas. But above all I need to get information from the family. It's impossible that no family member could know a thing about this, or at least some of them not have good guesses. I hope you will prepare yourself to answer me with perfect candor. Otherwise, my firm cannot do the job assigned to us."

"I aim to help any way I can, Mr. Dobbs."

"It may involve matters you consider personal," he said in that raspy voice, almost like a threat. Then, as if to soften the prospect, he added, "You understand that everything is confidential. I am not a judge of morals or anything else. I am after the facts. I am something of a psychologist. I understand human motivation, a talent which is indispensable in my work. What you tell me, I will never reveal without your permission, but it may be valuable in solving a mystery."

"I'll sure help any way I can, Mr. Dobbs."

"All right. Also, I would like for you to go through all the old photographs you own and be prepared to let me have the best and most recent picture of your father. I'll call you in about a week."

They hung up.

The water leak in the front yard had probably been there several days before he noticed it; he let it go another three days just because he didn't want to accept the messy job. Helen said, "George, somebody has squirted a lot of water on our lawn. It's mushy and squishy out toward the sidewalk. Did we leave the sprinklers on too long?"

"No. I don't turn the sprinklers on at all. It just encourages the grass to grow faster. We have a leak in the main inlet pipe, under the house or up toward the front faucet."

He was serious about no longer using the sprinkler system. The lawn was an issue to him, but too petty to talk about. They had a corner lot, and he could see up and down the street both ways the tailored lawns with perfect edging along the sidewalks, more like a park than a place to live. He could imagine some of the neighbors, any of them, looking out their window curtains and saying, "Look at that grass of Woodstock's! Some of it five or six inches high! And dandelions!" They didn't actually say anything, but he could guess what they were thinking. That's living in town, in a "nice" section—it's everybody else's business what you do in your own yard. Well, the neighbors were just going to have to put up with his messy yard.

Helen asked "Are you going to call the plumber?"

"I don't know. The last plumber I called for the little bathroom cost me four-hundred dollars and still didn't fix it the way I wanted. Forget the plumber. I'll dig the mess out and stop the leak when I get around to it."

He had meant to watch a baseball game but realized that the leak was adding up the water bill and he needed to dig a drainage ditch to let the ground dry out before he could explore for the leak. Starting at a low spot in the lawn with a long-handled spade, he began to dig. The gummy soil stuck to the spade. He got his big masonry trowel out of the junk in the garage, after a lot of hunting, to clean the shovel with. The muck stuck to the trowel too and had to be slung loose.

The roots and runners of the St. Augustine grass would not turn loose of the shovels full of gummy earth he pried up. The spade was dull. He took it to the back yard where a hose was hooked up, washed it clean, and sharpened it with a file. By jumping on it with both feet he could cut the grass runners and the hedge roots, then scrape and sling loose the mud. His ditch progressed toward the house, and a trickle of water began to run down it.

In the middle of his disgust from working in the gummy

mess, a strange question came to him: Why was he doing this? Trying to prove something about his age? Too stingy to hire a younger man who was supposed to be a professional plumber? Trying to prove something to his father? Trying on purpose to take on a task which would occupy his mind and take it away from the confused mess out west on the ranch? He had no answer, but felt certain that Papa would have done it himself in order to be sure it was done right.

As dusk came on, it was clear that the leak came just outside his own faucet and cut-off. The idiot city water people should be responsible; he could not even cut off the water so the leak would stop. They would stick him on the water bill and the repair both. He examined the cast iron cover on the city's water meter out by the sidewalk and decided that he could make a key himself and open it and cut off the water any time he got damned good and ready, stopping the meter from adding up the bill. But the trickle of water in his ditch suggested that he was only cursing pennies.

Back at the messy job of the water leak two days later, he contemplated the problem of shutting off the water. If he called the water department people, they would send a man with a simple key to the manhole where the water meter was located and where the water could be cut off from the street main. But he needed the water cut off and on several times while he dug and repaired the leak. He could see the bureaucrat water man standing around for hours, holding his damned key, drawing good money for doing nothing.

George brought out to the meter cover a quarter-inch rod which had been used as a poker in the back-yard barbecue grill, a small anvil, a bastard file, and a ball-peen hammer. In fifteen minutes he had made a key, which, with some time of tentative twisting and feeling, opened the manhole cover and exposed the official meter and cut-off. With a large set of vise-grips he turned off the water.

He went into the house to check for sure that it was off. Fortunately, Helen was gone on one of her outings with two or three other women in their sixties, doing what evidently seemed fun to them—taking a gang of kids from some orphanage, three station wagons full, to a zoo or something and for a picnic in the park. It had occurred to George a few times that what Helen really wanted was to play grandmother. Their grandkids were scattered, two in Houston and three in Tulsa, and it seemed like they were always in school or their parents were too busy to visit. Of course, he had to admit that he was usually too busy too.

Another hour of digging in the gummy earth, and he found the suspected leak, a connection in the copper line just outside his own cut-off. His shirt and trousers and bare arms became muddy as he dug a good hole around the connection so that he could work on it. He was thinking that Walter or Clarence would never do such work. Clarence was too educated and Walter was above it. In fact Walter probably wouldn't even call the plumber; he would have some maintenance supervisor call the plumber. Now, Papa would have done the work himself. And Johnny, who had never worked for anybody but Papa, would have done the work himself.

Turning the water back on at the meter, he saw that the suspected connection was indeed squirting a thin stream.

He found a roll of bearing packing or valve packing string in the junk in the garage, a large string, years old, heavy with grease and graphite. With this, after turning off the water, he packed the connection, tightening it as far as he could by hand, then giving one half turn with a Stillson wrench. With the water pressure back on, the connection still leaked one drop every five seconds, according to his count. He began the process of adding more packing.

Turning the water off and on, especially turning on a faucet in the house to have nothing come out, must have started an unconscious train of thought, which turned into conscious memories. The first water for the ranch house he could remember was drawn from the drilled well, which was eighty-seven feet deep. There was a squeaking pulley and a fuzzy whitish rope. The bucket was maybe five inches in diameter, to fit the well casing, three or four feet long. On wash days Mother took many buckets of water for the wash pots and the tubs. Walter and Clara had three-gallon buckets, and he had a two-gallon syrup bucket to help carry.

Then Papa put a sucker rod and a hand pump on the well. It seemed wonderful that, with one stroke on the handle, water came gushing out the spout. They put a piece of pipe on the handle to lengthen it so even the smaller kids could pump.

Then Papa put up the first windmill, with a twenty-five barrel storage tank up on a platform, and piped water to the back porch. All you had to do was turn on the faucet. It was about the same time that Papa bought the radio and a wind charger to keep the batteries charged; they could listen to the news every day, and kids who got their chores and school lessons done could listen to Red Skelton or Fibber Magee and Molly or Lum and Abner or Amos and Andy.

Still later Papa brought in a water-well spudder and drilled another well and put in a second storage tank. At the same time he put in two bathrooms in the house and ran water to the bunkhouse. Also a sewage system with four septic tanks.

George had almost forgotten the old cistern, once filled from gutters around the ranch house. That had been filled in and abandoned when Papa rebuilt the back porch.

Anyway, the idea that you must have water as if it were automatic, taken for granted, as if it were a God-given right to everybody, seemed ironic in the face of what Papa had done to supply plenty of good water. Hell, of course we must have water. An African woman carrying forty pounds of water in a jar on her head knew that. The trouble is that people in this country are spoiled today; they want hot or cold, even ice water, on demand. They want automatic dishwashers and garbage disposals and automatic clothes washers and dryers; he could not remember when he had last seen a rub board or a clothes line.

On the third try at packing the connection he got it sealed so that it did not leak a drop. Suspecting that the break had been caused in the first place by shrubbery roots, he sneaked a full box of table salt from the pantry and poured it in the hole all around the connection. Better to have some fancy shrubs die than have another leak.

He would leave the drainage ditch and the big hole open until he got around to covering them up. If the neighbors didn't like the looks of it they could go jump in the lake. As he put the tools away and went in the house to clean up, he could imagine Papa eyeing his muddy hands and arms and clothes and saying, "Good job, George."

W. H. Dobbs called in the morning and drove up to the house in a late model Lincoln about two o'clock. Looking at the automobile and the man, George figured he must draw good fees, plus expenses, for his work. Dobbs, who wore thick horn-rimmed glasses, settled himself in an easy chair in the front room, refused a cup of coffee, opened his briefcase, and got right down to business.

"First, Mr. George Woodstock, I must tell you I've already been to the ranch. What is your opinion or guess as to where your father is right now."

George said, "I don't have any guess. I can't figure it

out. I helped with the search a little, but I don't know any place he could be."

"Do you believe he is dead, or that he is in the ranch area, or that he has left the area?"

"I've got no idea."

"Did he have the energy and initiative to travel some distance?"

"He did the last time I saw him, but he was getting old. He always used to have a lot of energy."

"What type of man was he? Describe him."

"Well, maybe you know from Walter that he came out there before the turn of the century with his father and brother. Land was cheap. He did a lot to build up the ranch."

"Tell me more. What was he like?"

"Well, he was a hard worker and practical. Easygoing. He always got along with the hands if they would work. He was his own best hand. He didn't say, 'Go out there and do so and so.' He said, 'Come on. Let's go do so and so.' I've seen him ride out in a blizzard many a time back fifty years ago."

"Do you believe that he was intelligent?"

"Hell yes, I do. He would surprise you. He could do nearly anything he tried to do. He was practical and liked to work with his hands instead of going by books. Actually, he was a lot like me. I mean practical. Not educated, but he could figure out anything he needed to figure out."

Dobbs said in his raspy voice, "If he did not like books, how does it happen that he has such a huge, beautiful library out there on the ranch?"

"Oh, I didn't mean that he doesn't like books. He reads. He went to high school. He reads sometimes when he doesn't have anything practical he has to do. That library he got mostly for looks and for the use of other people."

"You say your father was a lot like you?"

"Yes, I'm sure he was. Or, I mean is."

"Well, he must have been a peculiar, or I should say unusual, man. I've got some answers, at least preliminary answers, from your two sisters and your two brothers. Each of you says that he was "just like me." Is that possible, Mr. George Woodstock?"

George laughed, thinking of Walter or Irma doing the sweaty, dirty work Papa had always done. "They are mistaken, Mr. Dobbs."

"Did he have a will disposing of his property at his death?"

"I don't know."

"Who would know?"

"Maybe a lawyer out there at the town of Woodstock. If Papa wrote it out by himself maybe nobody would know."

W. H. Dobbs was scribbling notes on a pad. He seemed to settle himself as if for a new attack. "Now, I want you to consider my next question carefully. You may resent it. Your tendency will be to just sidestep it. Here it is: Which ones of your father's children or grandchildren would benefit if he were missing? Which ones would benefit if he had made a will and didn't have a chance to change it? Who might benefit if there were no will? I'm not suggesting foul play. I'm asking who might not tell the whole truth. Please remember that anything you tell me is confidential."

George was taken aback. He *did* resent the question. "I don't think there's any such thing at all like you're getting at."

"Do you resent the question?"

"Hell no, I guess you're just trying to do your job. Look, Mr. Dobbs, we're just a kind of average family, some good and some bad in the whole bunch. But I'll tell you one thing for sure: not a one of Papa's kids or grandkids or great-grandkids but what wants to find him as quick as possible and see that he's taken care of."

"Please let me judge motivation," the man said. "The

question is whether anyone would benefit financially or otherwise."

"Not that I know of."

"What was your own financial relationship with your father?"

"Nothing. None. I left home and went on my own in 1939." He was beginning to dislike Dobbs. Then, almost aggressively, he said, "I'll tell you a fact like you seem to want and see what you make out of it. Papa promised me a hundred thousand dollars to help build up my shop. For equipment and such. He knew my plans for a certain kind of shop and he agreed with me. So he promised me the money."

"Were there any witnesses to the promise?"

"No."

"Well, I would think you would appreciate having him located and in sound mind."

"That's about the size of it."

"All right, let us leave the family for a moment. Has there been anyone in the past who might hold a grudge against your father on account of a business deal or for any other reason? Anyone who might believe that they have been cheated or insulted?"

"No, I don't think so."

"Your brother Walter mentioned some land deals back in the mid-1930s. Is there anyone who might feel cheated or believe that he broke his promise?"

"Look, Papa never cheated anybody in his life. In the '30s he was better off than most because he worked hard and was a good manager. You know how low beef went in the Fort Worth stockyards? In '34 some cutters and canners, what they make baloney and wienies out of, got down to seventy-five cents a hundred. That's three-fourths of a cent a pound. Some people couldn't pay their mortgages. Papa bought some land adjoining his as low as ten dollars an acre. I know one man tried to make a deal with him. The man couldn't pay the bank and he couldn't buy back the land and he wanted Papa to hold his note, which wasn't worth a red cent."

"Is that man still around? What was his name?"

"I don't know his name. He loaded up his family and went to California. Look, Papa never cheated anybody in his life, but if you think a man can build up a big ranch without looking after his own interests, you're mistaken."

"Do you think he ever told any lies in his business dealings?"

"No, I don't. He leased some land once to some oil drilling outfit without telling them it had already been drilled and come up with dry holes, but he said it was their business to know what they were doing. And I think so too."

Dobbs was fiddling around in his briefcase as if adjusting something, but George could not see what it was because the open lid was in the way.

"Now, Mr. George Woodstock, to a couple of other descendants. "Who is this Homer?"

"You mean Clara's grandson?"

"That's what I mean."

"He's just a weak-minded boy, maybe fourteen or sixteen years old, who has always gone out to the ranch a lot. He's retarded actually."

"Who is Annie?"

"That's another one of Clara's grandkids, maybe eight. She liked to go out to the ranch and Clara took her out there."

"What about Annie's mother? What was the relationship?"

"Well, I don't know that it makes any difference. Clara was not always practical or good in schoolwork, but she was always full of life. This is not important, but it was a daughter-in-law and mother-in-law thing. They did not always get along, but they didn't make any trouble about it. Clara spoiled little Annie."

"Would it be your judgment that Homer and Annie were your father's favorite grandchildren or great-grandchildren?"

"Well, yes. What I mean is they were handy when he got old. They were out there a lot. One time I came in, and Papa was down on his hands and knees on the rug, and Clara was holding Annie on his back like he was a horse; she was about two years old then. And Homer was making sounds like a mule or donkey braying. Papa was just trying to entertain them."

"Then I believe you would say that Homer and Annie were his closest kin during the past several years? Is that correct?"

"I suppose so. But, look, they are just kids. I hope you won't ask them a bunch of questions. There is no way they could know anything. I don't know what all your questions are about, but Homer and Annie don't know anything that would help you in your work."

"Who are Izzy and Johnnie?"

"Izzy is the ranch cook. After Mother died Papa had a lot of trouble with men cooks just hired a few weeks a year. He was expanding the ranch and had to hire a bunch of hands twice a year. Then he needed a housekeeper and somebody to take care of the garden and orchard and chickens and milk cow and such as that. She is a hard working woman."

"And Johnnie?"

"Well, you know that he is her son. He grew up on the ranch and took to the work. He's the best cowhand Papa ever had and he's a good ranch manager."

"Is there any possibility that he is your father's illegitimate son?"

"No. No."

"All right. You were going to search and find me a good recent photograph of Franklin Woodstock."

George took two four-by-six prints he had placed on top of the stereo and handed them over. "This is all I could find. I looked through everything we have. They are not too recent."

Dobbs took a six-inch magnifying glass out of his briefcase and peered at the pictures, obviously displeased.

George said, "That one on horseback is only about ten years old. Maybe fifteen. He's the one on the dun horse."

"And his face is in the shade of his big hat," Dobbs observed. "These pictures are worthless for identification."

"The other one is a snapshot of a painting. Clara talked him into sitting still long enough for this painter to do it."

"An artist's concept," Dobbs said. "Can you give me any explanation as to why the original painting hangs today in Izzy's bedroom? If there was nothing between her and Franklin Woodstock, why is the painting in her bedroom?"

"Well, I didn't know it was. She's a tender-hearted woman, always trying to take care of everybody. I guess after Papa went to the nursing home she was there in the big house by herself a lot, so she took the picture for company."

"Allow me to say, Mr. George Woodstock, that for an average American family you people are remarkably ignorant about your father. No one even has a good recent photograph of him. Can you tell me this: How tall was he?"

The questioning was becoming obnoxious. "I don't know. Maybe five-ten."

"Congratulations," Dobbs said sarcastically. "I have answers all the way from five-eight to over six feet. According to his army discharge in 1919, he was indeed five-ten."

The man said he had to go. He had an appointment to talk to Irma's son in Denver the next day. He declined to stay for supper. As he snapped the large briefcase shut, he said, as if it were incidental, "You understand that I have recorded our conversation. This does not at all invalidate my statement that everything is confidential."

Later George wondered what all he had said. He asked Helen, who had overheard some of the talk, but she could not remember whether he had said anything he should not have to this damned character who seemed more like an intruder than an employee of the family.

CHAPTER SIX

Irma

PAPA had been gone a month or more, and the problem would not let George rest. Irma called from Atlanta, upset about the way the entire matter was being handled, especially about Walter's plan for dividing the ranch into ten-acre plots.

"George," she said, "can't you do something? We depend on you. I do believe Walter wants to find Papa dead, so he can take charge. You know that I am a very spiritual person, but I want to be reasonable."

"There's no reason to get upset about the land," he told her. "The thing right now is to find Papa."

"I think I have an idea about that too. George, I need to talk to you."

"I'm listening," he said, aware that it was her long-distance call.

"No. I have to see you. There are so many things. Papa was a born-again Christian, you know. He was like me in so many ways. Our son Wilbur—you know the one who went to the seminary—he has left his regular pulpit and become an evangelist. Papa would be so proud of him. We have to see you and talk to you about the estate and about finding Papa. About blocking Walter."

"Well, Irma, I'm busy with my machine shop, but it would sure be nice for you all to come and see us."

"I want you to take us out to the ranch. Could you pick us up at the airport and take us out there? Please, George."

She was still his little sister, four years younger. Or fifty years ago she had been four years younger, and he had felt protective. He now felt like a sucker, but said okay. She would call him next week and let him know when.

He said, "Listen, Irma, I'm not going to hunt a parking place out at that airport and go in and wait, then try to find my car again. You'll have to call me after you arrive and be waiting in front of whatever airline office you come in on, with your bags. Then I'll pick you up."

He did not need another trip west right now unless there was something he could do in the search. But he could understand Irma's concern. Once she had been the baby of the family. Her manner now was anything but that of a baby.

As if he did not have enough to keep him busy, trying to get the shop straightened out, trying to get some work out of the new man Wiggins, hauling his brothers and sisters around, thinking about Papa, out of a clear blue sky some kind of bone scientist from Harvard University called on the evening after he talked to Irma.

The man's name was Overstreet. He said, "Mr. Woodstock, your brother Walter referred me to you. He suggested that, since you live there in the vicinity, you would be able to give me some information and perhaps cooperation. You are the brother of Walter; is that correct?"

"That's right."

"Well, I was one of Dr. A. S. Romer's students. He was world-famous for his fossil finds, and he operated in the general area of Woodstock as early as the late 1920s. Many of the old-time settlers in the region of northwest Texas knew him and respected him. The fossils of dinosaurs he recovered can be seen in museums around the world, and he made important contributions to the science of paleontology."

"What did Walter want you to talk to me about?"

"Well, I want you to understand, Mr. Woodstock, that the region of northwest Texas we are speaking of is very unusual from a geological and paleontological standpoint. There are washed-out areas called the 'redbeds.' They go back to the Permian period, some two-hundred and fifty million years ago. The various strata are amazingly close together. I understand that you grew up there. Do you recall the spots called the 'redbeds'?"

"We called them alkali flats."

"That's it. They are a red clayish material with a chemical composition such that grass will hardly grow. There is a particularly interesting spot of a few acres below a formation which the local people used to call Dead Cowbones Bluff. Do you know of that?"

"Yes. What did Walter want you to talk to me about?"

"Well, there is a project in the planning stage. A team of scientists including at least one anthropologist, one geologist, and one paleontologist may wish to survey and dig below that formation this summer. There are excellent chances of getting a generous grant from a foundation if the project can go forward."

"Look, Mr. Overstreet. Professor Overstreet. We have a problem down here about private family affairs right now, and it may last all summer. I don't think you'll be able to do your project at all this year."

"But, Mr. Woodstock, we are especially careful not to cause any trouble to land owners. And it would be a great contribution to science. There are important possibilities. I think it would not be a detriment to the Woodstock ranch to be a famous site."

"This is a private family trouble," he said. "I don't think you can do your project at all this year."

He finally got rid of the man.

Something about the whole proposition irritated him. He knew it didn't make sense, but it was as if this Overstreet was in with that confounded detective, and they agreed that Papa was an old fossil. George realized that he was not thinking straight. Too much on his mind.

He had found that he could trust Fowler to do any kind of work without supervision, but not the newest man, Wiggins. The man sometimes did not know what he was doing, but went ahead and did it anyway, then acted hurt if criticized. One nearly unforgivable thing he had done: drilled a half-inch hole in a drill press table. If it had been a new machine or one in good condition, George would have fired him on the spot. It looked like Wiggins might not last long. But then, an employee ought to be given a decent chance; everybody ought to be *good* for something.

It haunted him that his shop concerns, the need for money, tied in with the disappearance of Papa. Walter's big schemes sure would not return any money to anybody soon. Though he did not welcome wasting time with Irma, maybe they could at least agree to vote against their older brother's plans.

At the airport George found that Irma and her son had a pile of five bags, which filled up the trunk and half of the back seat of the Pontiac.

"George," she said, "we would love to visit with Helen, but I think we should go on and leave. I called Izzy and told her we will be there for supper."

Helen had said she really didn't want to go. They drove west. Irma was not much like her blowzy elder sister Clara. Irma, with her long upper lip and gray hair piled on top of her head, looked more like an Austrian aristocrat than a small-town grandmother. George once had thought she was different because she was the spoiled baby of the family. Her son, Wilbur, was an overweight, over-dressed man who seemed to have a permanent smile on his face. He looked as if he had eaten many rich Sunday dinners with the members of his congregation and had enjoyed them.

Fighting the Saturday traffic on the freeways, George broke into the chatter of his sister and nephew. He said, "Sis, you mentioned that you might have some clue about where Papa went."

"I do. I do. I have prayed over it, George. But there is so much to explain so that we can understand it. Papa was a born-again Christian, you know. That Walter, he said, 'Baloney.' I was never so hurt in all my life. We all know very well that Papa was a good Christian. Isn't that right?"

George did not want to be too much intimidated by her, especially if she avoided answering his question. "I heard that he said he was born again just to get old Brother Biggs off his back. I didn't think he was ever baptized."

"Why of course he was baptized! You know he used to offer thanks at the table nearly every meal we ate."

"That was when Mother was alive."

"The point is that he was a real Christian at heart, George."

"I don't deny that he was. He was the best man I ever knew. You mentioned that you might have some clue about where Papa went."

"That's why I wanted to talk about what kind of man he is. He was always very spiritual. One time he spoke to me about the piney woods of East Texas. It was in the big room by the fireplace. I was already graduated from OU and was in social work, but had come home to see him. You know Grandpa had come from East Texas and had some kinfolks there, and they went back to visit a few times. So Papa spoke about the tall trees. He said it was like a temple. As a boy, he had stood in the forest and worshipped God among the tall trees that point to heaven. He said it was like a temple.

"So, George, I feel sure he knew he was getting old, you know. Everyone gets old. I believe he wanted to go back to what he remembered that he thought was sacred, to see it again before he passes away from this earth. He was sentimental and very spiritual. If I were that old I might want to go back to the ranch and look at the stars and the prairie."

"Then I suppose you told Dobbs, the detective, about this East Texas thing. He said he might have to search east and west both."

"I certainly did. But why would Papa want to go west to New Mexico? That's silly. The detective person asked me a lot of silly questions and one that was certainly insulting."

"How's that?"

"You know what he asked? He asked if it is possible that Johnny is Papa's illegitimate son!"

"He asked me that too. I told him I didn't think so."

"I wish you had punched him in the nose. Imagine! To have relations with a cook! I was never so insulted in all my life. George, you may not know the exact words Mother said on her deathbed. Walter and I were there in the hospital in town with Papa. We were all away from home, all us kids. We knew she would die from the TB and all, but she lingered on and on. Walter and I happened to be there that last evening. Papa's words and Mother's are burned into my soul. She knew she was going. She said, 'You are young enough to marry again, Frank. I'm sorry to leave you.' He said, 'No, Amy. no. I can't think of any woman but you.' It was a sacred promise. I guess, the only time I ever saw Papa cry. Those were the last words she heard on this earth. It was a holy time and a sacred promise. Knowing Papa, I know he kept his promise exactly."

George had negotiated all the idiot freeway signs and the Saturday traffic and now he lined the old Pontiac out westward.

She went on. "We must make the land where we grew up a shrine and a memorial to the godly life that Papa led. I want Wilbur to explain how important it is, but first I want to explain the basic idea. It doesn't matter if we find Papa quickly or later. What I'm talking about is to recognize his long life. We can find him if we search east, but it doesn't matter, except to take care of him. Which we must. But, George, we should make a religious retreat out of the ranch, a place for good Christians to come and enjoy good wholesome recreation and enjoy fellowship and listen to gospel preaching.

"You'd be surprised at how successful such places are, George. It will pay for itself if we furnish the land. I've been to the one in Tennessee. It was just like a big beautiful picnic every day and a blessing to everybody. We could get the best preachers to come, like Falwell and Billy Graham and Robison and Swaggert and Oral Roberts, to visit and hold services, and people could bring their unsaved kinfolks and camp out till everybody was saved."

George knew that she was looking at him for approval. He kept his eyes on the highway and said, "I thought you were mad at Walter because he wants to use Papa's land for something before he's dead. Like he was already dead and willed it to us."

"It's not the same. This is not the same at all. Papa would be proud of this plan. What Walter has is a scheme to make money. But the religious retreat is more important than I have even mentioned. Wilbur has consulted with scientists and all kinds of experts. You'll be surprised at the name of the project. It fits so well. We are talking about things that are predicted in the holy Bible. Explain the plan, Wilbur. Like you have been working on. Wilbur?"

Her son, the evangelist, may have dozed off in the back seat, but he became alert immediately. He said, "The two plans mesh together perfectly, the religious retreat and the more urgent haven of safety. In today's world one threat overshadows all others."

"Tell him the name you have, Wilbur."

"Noah's Ark. It's not a simple threat we have and it's not a simple solution, but the answer is Noah's Ark. The Bomb will come. Mankind has never invented a weapon of destruction without finally using it. God has revealed his secrets to mankind so that they may destroy themselves and fulfill his prophecy.

"The whole thing sounds strange at first, Uncle George, even silly, until a person thinks about it a while. Think of all the troubles around the world. Suppose Russia and America make good treaties and act in a responsible manner. Treaties have been broken before. Other countries have the Bomb, and more will get them. Think of all the evil people around the world, leaders, who would rather start Armageddon than not get their way. Hitler sure would have. We can think of many more. They will find reasons. If America would use the bomb in 1945 for a good purpose, a dozen other countries will use it when they get ready.

"Uncle George, the complicated thing is what happens when the Bomb comes and afterward. I have studied it intensively and have been consulting with experts. We even know some plans for protection by the Russians. But the first thing we have to understand is that the whole world will be involved. This is one world now. All these alliances and treaties and ties. Some evil dictator will even shoot a hydrogen bomb on Moscow, so they will retaliate against us.

"There are two words, Uncle George, the experts keep bringing up: interdependence and anarchy. We all depend on each other just to get by. People think they can tune in the radio or TV when the bombs are falling, but the electricity will be dead or the announcer and technician will be running for the country. They think they can go to the hospital, but the doctors will be trying to save their kids and grandkids. The phone will be dead. The water supply will be cut off or dangerous from radiation. The trains won't run. The busses won't go. The planes won't fly. Because the drivers and pilots will be taking care of their own urgent business. The governors will call out the National Guard, but they won't come. The policemen and firemen will be trying to escape. The street lights won't work. There will be no medicine and no ambulances. All this is because of the interdependence of people today.

"It will be anarchy, Uncle George. Some honest man will feel he has a right to break a window and go in a grocery store to get milk for his baby. Some honest man may feel he has a right to siphon gas out of a parked truck to put in his car and save his family. The next thing we know: widespread looting and rioting. Within a week people will be starving. The dead from blast and fire and radiation, that won't be half of it. Starvation! Then the plagues from bad water and bad sewer systems and dead bodies. Nobody can survive in the big population centers."

"Tell him the saddest part about Noah's Ark, Wilbur."

"The saddest part is a thing we have wept over and prayed over. Guns. Every member of Noah's Ark over fifteen years of age must have a rifle and plenty of ammunition. Those people without forethought, those unprepared, Christian or non-Christian, will try to take away from us what God has led us to set aside. Secular justice, by which we mean the law officers and judges who are worldly, will do us no good; we must go back at that time to the harsh justice like God in the Old Testament. We will have stored at Noah's Ark at least a thousand rounds for every weapon, for there will be a need, not only in the first sad days and weeks, but for many years yet to come. That ammunition must be stored properly and not wasted.

"Uncle George, each member will be responsible to get to the refuge at that time. Every person must decide on a route and store up some gasoline and whatever he needs to get his family to the refuge. He will be admitted to the ranch on positive identification by three other members. In those days and weeks of death and anarchy maddened and desperate people will flock to the countryside, trying to find a haven, begging and pleading in vain. But they did not have foresight. Farmers and ranchers will fight them in order to save their own food supply and their health and safety. There will be guerrilla warfare over the width and breadth of the land."

"Tell your uncle how it will be at the ranch, Wilbur."

"We will have a powerful radio transmitter. Every fifteen minutes we will transmit, 'The Ark is ready to float. The Ark is ready to float.' The members will pick it up with battery radios, and it will give them faith and strength and confidence."

To George the whole thing sounded about as far out as Walter's plan. He said, "Don't you think, Sis, that we should concentrate right now on trying to find Papa?"

"I certainly do. Everybody must search to the east. Somewhere he may be helpless and alone. But Wilbur wants to contact some local people and discuss the combination of the religious retreat and Noah's Ark. It is important at this time to get moving on these projects, at least to let people know the problem and the possibilities so that we can do what is right and necessary after everybody has thought it over. Wilbur, explain what we must have at the ranch. You'll be surprised at how much planning Wilbur has already done."

"Well, Uncle George, it's obvious that we need a good supply of food that will keep, like dried beans and dried raisins and canned goods and things. We need to generate our own electricity. We will have to have a large tank, or several tanks, of gasoline to operate the generators and tractors and trucks, to last while the members get used to the new life. We will need plenty of warm clothing and raincoats, because our boundaries will have to be patrolled every day of the year by armed men. We will soon depend on wood and cow chips for fuel, for Mom has told me that we have three or four miles of Plum Creek on the ranch with large trees. We can also use the scrub mesquites. That means we need chain saws and then axes and grinders to sharpen the axes.

"We are going to need experts who can fix it so we don't depend on the outside. We need doctors. We don't need lawyers; they can be replaced by good fellowship and wise leaders."

Irma interrupted. "Wilbur will probably be the first president."

"We need people who know how to grind wheat into flour, Uncle George, and corn into meal. I confess I don't know how. I hope I'm humble enough to admit it. We need men who can fix a windmill, whether to pump water or provide power, and they must be able in the years to come to replace worn-out metal parts with wooden parts. Mom has pointed out how useful you would be in the total picture."

George was thinking that the nephew, who had a peculiar habit of smiling even when he talked about serious things, had thought about his project a lot. But he had not said a word about finding his grandfather, Franklin Woodstock.

Wilbur went on. "We must store seeds, animal and vegetable. I mean wheat and maize and corn and peaches and everything. Then we must have horses and cows and sheep and chickens, male and female, and donkeys and work oxen and turkeys and goats, and even camels, male and female, every animal of use to man. It may be necessary to make underground stables for use when radiation is bad, so we can save the pairs of seed animals, male and female. That's where we got the idea for the name of the whole plan, Noah's Ark."

George was glad to see the city limits of the little town of Woodstock ahead.

Irma took up the harangue. "It's so good to have the opportunity to put the whole plan before you, George. It's so much to think about. I'm sure you will want to think long and hard before you sign up to be a member. But,it is not something we can put off forever. We must have forethought and have everything arranged. Too late is just too late, that's all.

"The ranch is the ideal size for the religious retreat and Noah's Ark both. You can see the way Wilbur has it planned we need room to survive. And the ranch is far enough away from big cities. You know, people realize that it's not as sinful out in the country as it is in the city. The plan will pay for itself. Wilbur says if he is the president he doesn't want a big salary, just a reasonable salary. I told him a hundred thousand a year, and you know what he said? Sixty thousand! Many people will serve free and donate things like supplies and machinery."

At the old home Izzy welcomed them with open arms. She had fixed a beef brisket and laid a supper fit for a king. Irma and Wilbur, after eating, said that they needed to see some people in town. George declined to drive them, but let them take the Pontiac.

He chatted with Johnny and the two tenant farmer-cowhands. Besides doing the regular work around the place, they were still combing the twelve square miles of the place for evidence that Papa had been there. Homer had been "helping" them. Johnny was trying, with limited success, to teach him to stay in the saddle on Old Baldy. Homer tried to take part in the bull session, but hardly said anything which could be understood.

About bedtime, George found out that he was more of a sucker than he had realized. Irma and Wilbur came in and announced that Wilbur would fill the pulpit of the First Baptist Church on the following day, for both morning and evening services. George had not been consulted, but it was taken for granted that he would furnish them an automobile and would drive them back to the Metroplex whenever they decided to go. He called Helen collect and told her about the developments.

CHAPTER SEVEN

Homer and Annie

GEORGE wondered about the kerosene lamp in the big room where the library was now. He could see its glow all the way down the hall, like a small night light, a touch of the old before-electricity days which Papa had always liked. Surely Izzy or Johnny watched the lamp to make sure it was safe. There were two lamps on the mantel, but usually only one was lit. What if someone carelessly set a stack of books on the mantel and they slowly toppled over and upset the lamp?

It was almost as if he were looking for an excuse not to go to sleep, in fact to go and look at the big room where he had sat as a boy by the big fireplace and listened to the wonderful new radio Papa had bought.

He found the worn brown robe he had left in the closet two or three years before, put it on, then went silently down the hall to the door of the library. Someone was there. He could make out the youngster Homer. Instead of sitting in one of the big chairs, Homer sat in a cane-bottom straight chair under the lamp. He held some object on his knees and held his face down near it, as if searching with his eyes.

When he realized what the object was, George first thought, *No wonder he has trouble with his eyes—trying to squint at pictures and print in a book under such poor light.* Then George remembered their old understanding about the boy. Homer knew he was different, that he was missing something. The boy had seized upon the idea that the answer must be in books, that because he could not read he could not be like others.

He felt a surge of pity for the persistent young man, who seemed to believe that somehow there is a secret in the mysterious marks on a printed page. That people stare at them carefully and it makes them normal. That because he had not opened enough books, looked at the small marks, put his finger on them as he looked, he remained different. But that he must persist in search of the secret, and that some day, or in the middle of the night, the answer might come.

There were two scandals concerning Homer, though the second had been hushed up and had become an uncertain matter.

First, he had been kicked out of school in the third grade. Several times he had been sent home for arguing with the teacher, for standing up when she said, "Sit down," and for trying to talk his clumsy talk when she said, "Be quiet."

"It disturbs the other pupils," the teacher said, "and distracts their attention; they giggle instead of reciting their lesson."

Three times the principal of Woodstock Grammar School had Ed and Pauline Bender in for a conference. The man insisted that he did not object that Homer was slow, but that the boy must be taught some semblance of discipline by his own parents. At the third conference the principal suggested psychiatric help and issued a solemn warning that he might be removed from school. Only a few days later the issue came to a head when Homer had an argument with the teacher, disputing incoherently what she said. He "threw a fit," the teacher said. Homer was expelled. His grandmother, Clara Woodstock Bender, wept over it for a week; she had always said that all her peculiar grandson needed was some education.

But Clara had been known as the "dingbat" by other family members since Walter gave her that tag fifty years earlier. She had lost her young husband at Omaha Beach in 1945 and been left with town property and with two little boys, Edwin and Freddy. Now she lived in the same small town where she had spent nearly all her life, was treated decently by her two sons but barely tolerated by her daughters-in-law, and spent much of her time thinking of ways to spoil Homer and another grandchild, Annie.

The second scandal about Homer had been only a strong suspicion among family members. A few months after he was expelled, the school library was broken into; according to the poor records of books they kept, about a dozen volumes were stolen. Amazingly, a month later another window of the school library building was broken, some intruder entered, another armload of books were stolen, but the first twelve were returned to their places on the shelves.

At that time Homer was often missing for hours at a time. He could not be found at home or at his grandmother's house on Third Street. But they had already noted the boy at various times staring at the Woodstock newspaper, sometimes holding it sideways or upside down.

The theft of library books went on for months. The school authorities could not afford to hire a night watchman. The sheriff, who liked to use big-city police words, said that the *modus operandi* was the same in all the break-ins, so there was only one criminal. But since the villain always brought the books back, he could only be charged with breaking and entering.

Whether the old patriarch, Franklin Woodstock, bribed any authorities was never known by the family, but the old man began to add to his library and insisted that his peculiar great-grandson spend a lot of time out at the ranch. Then the break-ins at the school stopped.

The old man went wild buying books. He brought in a cabinet maker and added two walls of shelves in the big room. Mostly he bought sets, cheap but well-bound: Gibbons' *Decline and Fall,* a set called *The Harvard Classics, The History of Civilization* by the Durants, Catton's Civil War books, a long set in imitation buckram put out by the Classics Club. Homer spent hours holding the volumes, squinting at them.

The family believed that they understood all about the school library books, that it was fortunate that no one had got caught, that the matter had been well settled. But two years after the last school break-in someone broke into the county courthouse, went through the files of the County Clerk, used the office copying machine, and evidently took nothing. An opened drawer held stacks of dollar bills and change, but had not been disturbed. The sheriff thought it the same *modus operandi,* in the sense of being senseless.

The family could not account for Homer's whereabouts on the night of the courthouse job but could think of no rationale. With so many great books to stare at, why should the boy want to steal copies of county records? Maybe all the break-ins had been a matter of county politics or something. It remained a mystery.

Watching the motionless youngster peering intently over the volume in the dim lamplight, George felt an urge to help him if there was any way. Who could guess what strange mixture of hope and confusion turned in the mind of the nearly grown boy? Who could guess what kept burning in him to make him search in books, of all places? When his trouble lay in controlling his arms and legs and his tongue. And hearing people. To tell exactly what they said. And looking at the world to see it as it is.

George bumped one of the double doors against the door jam slightly and cleared his throat to get attention.

Homer did not look up. He put his hand over one ear, then put it over one eye. Then he put the hand over the other ear, then the other eye, as if trying to puzzle out the interruption. From the floor beside his chair the boy picked up an object which George had not noticed, a mirror about six inches square. Homer turned the pages of the book away from himself, clumsily, and stared at their reflection in the small mirror.

"Homer?" George said softly. "Homer, I saw you in here. I thought maybe I would help you. Maybe read something to you."

He stepped forward and reached for the book. The youngster clutched the volume to his chest. "Papa," he said, as if in defense, his face creased with fear and a frown.

"That's all right," George said, still feeling generous. He strolled along the rows of books, looking. It was impossible to read many titles in the poor light, and it seemed somehow impolite to turn on the electric lights when Homer had been satisfied with the kerosene lamp.

There were three or four shelves of law books. Suddenly an idea occurred to him: What if Homer had been trying to puzzle out a law book and someone had explained to him that it was a law book? Maybe it was connected with the courthouse break-in when the County Clerk's records were ransacked. Maybe the boy had picked up the idea that the law is in the courthouse, and something there would help him be able to read law books, and he would become normal like other people. So he had managed to copy some records to stare at later. The whole idea was far-fetched, but nobody else had ever found any explanation at all.

What he needed was something like *King Arthur and the Roundtable* or some of those books Horatio Alger Jr. used to write about young men getting ahead by hard work and honesty. George had not read much of anything for decades except the newspaper and tech manuals and specifications. He owned a thick volume called *Machinery's Handbook* with all kinds of valuable information and tables in it, and nearly every page he had marked with greasy finger prints in the margins.

It was hopeless to find anything in the shelves. He went back to the youngster. Homer, in an apologetic gesture, offered him the book. George took it briefly and managed to hold back a laugh when he saw the title: *Critique of Pure Reason,* by Immanuel Kant. It was some kind of philosophy or such. He did not want to try to understand it himself, much less try to explain it to the boy.

George said, "Well, time for me to get to bed." He left the boy sitting there with the book.

Walking down the hall in the dark, he wondered why he had not just asked Homer about the courthouse break-in instead of speculating about it.

Next morning Irma and Wilbur were busy getting dressed up to impress the locals in the church where he was to be the guest speaker. Irma was afraid that her Sunday hat had been damaged by the rough handling of her bags, but it was safely in the hat box and only required a bit of fussing and adjusting the ribbons.

They demanded that everyone must attend church with them. But Johnny had chores around the barn. George had no Sunday clothes with him. Izzy obviously had to clean up the breakfast dishes and fix dinner. As for Homer, they did not ask him, since one never knew when he might make a scene, and he did not look right. Homer's clothes did not fit; they looked too big in some places, too tight in others. Sometimes his shirt front was buttoned in the wrong holes. Sometimes one shoe was untied. It was hopeless to think of him in a Sunday tie.

George took a bucket of table scraps down to the old sow in her pen behind the milk cow barn. When he brought the bucket back, he said jokingly to Izzy, "Why didn't you all butcher that old hog in the winter? She would make a lot of soap."

With a twinkle in her black eyes she said, "We don't make soap. We're rich. We buy soap already made. That old hog will make a dozen pigs for next winter."

She was skimming sour cream from cans and crocks of clabbered milk, filling an old fashioned churn which used a wooden plunger. He said, "Let me churn, Izzy."

"You sure? It takes a long time."

"Yes. Please. I haven't churned butter in fifty years. Please."

"Okay. Don't go too fast. Don't raise the dasher out of the cream and it don't slosh out."

He sat in a straight chair and methodically churned up and down, thinking that certain women's work is very peaceful. Every evening and every morning before daylight she or Johnny milked two Jersey cows. God knew what they did with all the milk and butter. Gave some of it to Buck and Slim. Now she was putting some heated clabber in cheese-cloth bags, squeezing out the whey into the sink, making more clabber cheese.

"How will you eat all that cottage cheese?" he asked.

"Feed it to the *pollos*. They grow like weeds, eating grain and grasshoppers and clabber cheese. We'll have fryers in three weeks. Tell Helen to come out, and we'll clean a dozen fryers real good for her to put in her freezer. They're Rhode Island Reds."

"I'll ask her," he said. It was not a bad idea. Helen would get a kick out of helping Clara and Izzy to spoil Homer and Annie.

He was thinking that Izzy was actually a beautiful woman at about the age of sixty, but in no way like the Anglo models and starlets. Her ankles were thick, made for walking and carrying loads. George mused about standards of beauty. Churning methodically, he became aware that she looked at him. She stood with her arms hanging down. Two tears were running down her brown cheeks.

"They will find him, won't they, George? The detective will find him."

"I hope so, Izzy."

"I pray to Mary."

"I know you do. We can only hope."

"Sometimes it feels like he is here on the ranch somewhere, but Johnny searches and searches. I don't think he went east like Irma says, or west like Clarence said on the phone. He loved it here."

George said, "Please don't worry so much about it, Izzy. All we can do is search and hope and do our best." She seemed more like a sister, or even a mother, than a hired cook.

Clara phoned, interrupting the sentimental scene. When she found that Irma was in town, she immediately planned to come out to the ranch and bring granddaughter Annie to see her Great-aunt Irma. No invitation was needed.

George spent most of that morning, along with Homer, watching Johnny use his portable arc welder to repair and adapt the drawbar of an old John Deere tractor. Homer had to be constantly cautioned not to stare at the arc light. Johnny seemed to have complete patience with the boy. Apparently the job was a free one for the cowhand or tenant farmer Slim, who had insisted that he needed the tractor in working order the next day. George was thinking that Johnny had the right approach and initiative to be a partner in his tooling shop, with a few years of machine shop experience.

On the other hand, the young Hispanic already had more than a few years experience at what he was doing on the ranch. Some five years earlier George had seen him doing the castrating on a pen full of bull calves, one by one as they were roped and held down. Papa had sat on the fence and watched. Johnny's hands were deft and sure with the knife, leaving little or no dripping blood, as he had evidently been taught by Papa.

Irma and Wilbur did not have the forethought to call and say that they would have the noon meal with a deacon and his guests. But fortunately, Clara, her daughter-in-law Pauline, and her granddaughter Annie came just in time to eat. Izzy did not seem flustered by the uncertainty; she seemed to be used to it. There were juicy ham steaks, with peach pickles, and English peas and green onions fresh out of the garden and sour dough bread.

Clara had promised Annie that they would drive out to the Old Place where her Great-great-Papa had been a boy. Just for a few minutes.

But Pauline insisted that the child had to take a nap first. While the nap was supposedly going on, they heard giggling in the library and went in to find Homer on his hands and knees, pretending to be a horse. Annie was perched on his back with Papa's old Stetson hat hanging on her head. She probably would have gotten a spanking if her grandmother Clara had not been there.

By the middle of the afternoon the two women were in enough accord to drive out to the Old Place. George was satisfied to let them have the front seat of Clara's car while he sat in the back between the two youngsters. They drove out the road south toward the tenant farms, then turned off on the overgrown wagon road east toward the Woodstock homeplace of the turn of the century.

They had always called it the Old Place. George actually wanted to see it. Papa had built the present ranch headquarters about 1920. All that stood at the Old Place was a sagging gray barn. Lumber from the early house had been hauled away to patch cowlots, to make pig-pens, to split up for kindling wood.

A jackrabbit bounded away from the sound of the car, clearing low clumps of brush as if demonstrating his jumping ability. He stopped in the open a hundred yards from the road, pricked his ears straight up and watched. "That's mine! That's my rabbit!" Annie said, louder than necessary.

"Young lady!" Pauline said. "You quieten down that nonsense. Right now!"

A quarter mile from the Old Place they drove along a gentle slope which was covered with vivid wildflowers. Annie said to Homer, "Those are mine, but you can look."

Pauline fixed her with a fierce glance. "Young lady!"

"But they *are* mine, Mama. My Great-great-Papa gave them to me. Before he went to the nursing home."

"Are you going to start that will business again? I don't want to hear any more of it."

George was thinking that the woman was impolite and certainly spoiling what was supposed to be a short pleasure drive. At about where the old front yard had been, Clara parked. Pauline insisted there were rotten planks with rusty nails in them all around, and they should not walk around.

They stood near the car, possibly trying to imagine Papa living here as a boy. George happened to note that Annie was looking at the sky. A hawk circled lazily on the late spring up-drafts. The little girl saw that he had seen and pointed briefly to herself. Seeing that the mother was not watching, he pointed at the hawk and nodded and pointed at the girl. Annie giggled quietly at being understood.

Heading back, Clara drove down around the Old Place tank, a body of water that covered two or three acres. It had been the first one built on the ranch. George remembered that there had always been tank building or planning. Papa believed that cows grazed more evenly if they did not have to walk more than a half mile, or a mile at most, to water. There were ten or twelve tanks on the land today, their earth dams made at first with mules pulling slips or fresnos, later with tractors. The faces of the dams were ship-lapped with thin slabs of rock. The water was usually murky, reddish brown. Around them grew scattered willows, even cottonwoods, and at some places in the shallows tule and cattail reeds.

They stopped a few minutes near the water. Annie and Homer walked down toward some still backwater where cattails grew. The girl pointed among the reeds and Homer peered. She was saying something to him. George thought he was sure that she was pointing at a tadpole or a frog, saying it was hers.

When they got back to the car Homer had mud on his shoes. Clara drove them on back to the ranch house without another stop.

Again Irma and her son Wilbur did not bother to call, but showed up about ten o'clock. Early in the morning, driving back east, George listened silently to their talk. Many good Christian people, they said, had shown interest in their ideas about a Christian retreat and the Noah's Ark. George did not invite them home but took them directly to the airport and dumped them at the curb with their five bags. Then he headed for his shop to see how things were going.

CHAPTER EIGHT

Labor Troubles

HE was sharpening some drills by hand on a pedestal grinder when the private investigator Dobbs called. There was no mistaking the raspy voice of the man. And when he was addressed as Mr. George Woodstock, it seemed a safe bet that the call was being recorded and tagged with a full name so that it could be studied later.

"Mr. Woodstock, we need to get your opinion or best guess on an important matter. You have heard your father talk about moving north or at least visiting to the north. Is that right?"

"I don't know what you mean, Mr. Dobbs."

"I'm talking about an elderly person dwelling on an idea. He has missed something in his life that he always wanted to do. He sees that he is getting old, so he goes to complete his life, so to speak."

"What's that got to do with going north? Papa never especially wanted to go to the big cities up north."

"We are not talking about big cities, Mr. George Woodstock. We are talking about Wyoming and Montana and such. Did not your father talk about the old days of cattle driving north out of Texas? Did not he mention that the summers are cooler on the northern plains?"

"Well, I guess he did, but he also used to talk about the mountains out west in New Mexico."

"That is not the issue at this time. I am calling from

Dodge City, Kansas, at this time. We have a dim lead. Suppose your father had come here. Where would he likely go next?"

"I don't know. It seems kind of far-fetched to me."

"What we have is a total situation that is far-fetched, as you say, Mr. George Woodstock. Let me explain the situation. My understanding is that Juan Woodstock knows the ranch area as well as anyone could and has been continually searching. We have interviewed every logical source around the town of Woodstock. Therefore we must search every lead, and we must have the cooperation of every kin and friend, and we must try to think of the motivation of Mr. Franklin Woodstock.

"Now we have been authorized by Walter Woodstock to offer a modest reward for information leading to discovery of the whereabouts of Franklin Woodstock, and we have offered a sum of five-hundred dollars here in Dodge City. A white-haired man about five feet, ten inches tall was here ten days ago. He was thought to have some ranching background, and one informant believed he had a Texas accent. Apparently he did not register at any motel.

"The city and county law officials here tell me there is considerable tourist trade through the town, so that many strangers pass through; however it is the best lead we have developed. We have to be ready under the circumstances to accept dim leads and follow them up. Now, supposing that it was your father, where might he have gone next? Denver? Sheridan? Where?"

"I don't have the slightest idea, Mr. Dobbs."

"Any opinion or memory you have may be of value. Any information is better than no information. If you think of anything he said about going north, we need to know. You see, this lead is important. I have checked out a half dozen old men who seemed to be nearly ninety in age in East Texas and New Mexico. Every lead must be checked out. If you can give me no suggestions, I shall proceed to North Platte, Nebraska.

"But, Mr. George Woodstock, as you realize, I am adding up an extensive long distance phone bill keeping in touch with all your brothers and sisters and the various third generation kin scattered over the country. One of Franklin Woodstock's grandsons is in Hong Kong and one granddaughter in Alaska. And, of course, these calls become a part of expenses which are added to our fees. Therefore, I will give you our headquarters number and ask you to call if you remember any kind of clue or locate any photograph useful for identification. I will be in touch with my headquarters daily."

George took down the number and was glad to be free of the raspy voice. He could have mentioned Papa's fling at catching mustangs back before the first World War, in Wyoming or Arizona or somewhere, trying to do what his own father had done; but what in the world did that have to do with the situation now?

The new hand, Wiggins, had been in an argument with Bob Fowler. It seemed that Wiggins had insisted on using a fly cutter in the Bridgeport mill to rough out a steel jig base. George asked him to come into the office. The man flopped into a chair and sat there looking mistreated.

"Mr. Wiggins," he said, as patiently as he could manage, "we have all worked in shops with better equipment and more machines. Now, that little Bridgeport is the closest thing we have to a jig bore machine. We hold tolerances of plus or minus one thousandth on hole locations. When you take a big cut with a fly cutter, it's just like pounding on the headstock bearings with a hammer every rpm."

"Well, I don't see why the hell I can't use the best machine when it ain't in use."

"I just told you. We use that old shaper to rough out steel. We keep the Bridgeport clean and oiled and take it easy on the ways and the headstock. Besides the shaper there's an old Cincinnati out there which is wired up."

"Well, I don't see why the hell you have a fly cutter if you don't use it. I get me a piece of tool steel sharpened right and get it set in the fly cutter, and Fowler tells me I can't do it."

"We have that fly cutter because I made it myself about ten years ago. You can take a cut in aluminum maybe a thirty-second. Or skim a steel cut maybe ten thousandths. No more. I expect you to follow the orders and suggestions of Bob Fowler."

When the man started to go out the office cubicle door, George asked, "By the way, Wiggins, where are my inside mikes?"

"Out yonder on a bench some place. I used them yesterday."

"Please put my tools back where you got them as soon as you are through with them. When will your personal tools be here from Detroit?"

"How in the hell do I know? I'm doing the best I can, if that Fowler will get off my back."

About six o'clock that afternoon, when everyone else had gone home, Fowler told him that Wiggins was saying that the shop workers needed a union in order to get decent treatment.

George said, "I don't think he's going to last long around here. By the way, Bob, I been looking over the records a little. We seem to be making money on everything you work on. I don't like guys to ask me for a raise, so we better go ahead and raise you to fifteen bucks an hour. That will be on your paycheck. Then we'll start keeping a record of three bucks an hour more, which you can only use to buy in if you stay here and I get the financing and we build the shop up and start the partnership plan with five working partners like I've been talking about. Is that all right with you?"

Fowler's grin looked about a foot wide. "I figured to wait a couple of months, George, to ask for a raise."

"Well, you know how it is here lately. I've got a hundred things on my mind, running back and forth to West Texas. You've done more to run the shop than I have the last month."

"Okay. Good deal."

George was confident that he knew how to set up a first-class job shop tooling outfit which would do good, dependable work for its customers and be profitable to its five working owners. If only his damned brothers and sisters would get their grabby hands off Papa's estate.

He was aware that he could have become a civil engineer or a mechanical engineer, that he could even now. But he had not been willing to put up with all their ideas about what a person should study for a degree. More important, he wanted to work with his hands, with steel, aluminum, brass, copper. With all the kinds of iron: the grades of cast iron, mild steel hot rolled or cold rolled, steel to be hardened from the cheapest to air hardening and high speed steel, the tough kind and the brittle, to make it patterned exactly so that it would serve. He felt sorry for people who had never held metal in their hands and known that they had made it accurate.

Years ago in a job shop he had made a three-stage progressive die for a small part. They ran it on a seventy-ton press. The customer told him a year later that the die had produced two million parts, with a few sharpenings, and looked good for some more millions. His head had been in the clouds, thinking about controlling that seventy tons exactly, making it cut, pierce, form metal. You cannot get that kind of satisfaction as an engineer sitting at a desk with a pencil in your hand.

That kind of satisfaction made it almost worthwhile to live in the crowded confusion around big cities. His plan for the ideal small tooling shop kept him from moving away out somewhere to the country or a small town.

Wiggins had a simple milling fixture he was supposed to be finishing up. They had a design: just a nest and clamps on the base, a couple of cutter setting blocks, and a flat go-no-go gauge. George asked the man whether the job would be ready to go out tomorrow when it was due. Wiggins said that it would not, that the set-blocks and go-no-go gauge had to be sent out to heat treat for hardening.

"That's a couple of days," George said.

"That's their problem. We ain't got no way to harden them here."

"You stick around a few minutes," George told him. "I want to show you something. It's our problem when one of our customers has a machine and an operator sitting idle two days because we didn't deliver a tool when we promised."

"It's quitting time."

"You can stick around a few minutes if you don't have anything to do right away."

The big back door was open. George brought in three fire bricks which had been stacked among the junk at the rear and a five-gallon can half full of used crankcase oil. He wheeled the oxygen and acetylene bottles to the open doorway, put a medium tip on the torch and adjusted the flame to a good hot blue. He got an oversize pair of pliers to use for tongs and settled himself flat on the dirty concrete floor.

Wiggins squatted, watching, halfway dubious, halfway bored.

George talked as he played the flame against one block, which was placed on a fire brick. "This is oil-hardening stuff. It has to slowly get cherry red. You have to go all around and stay off the edges and corners, or they'll melt. The idea is to heat it evenly and let it sort of soak cherry red a minute, but don't let it get yellow. That's about right."

He gingerly picked up the block with the pliers and dropped it into the oil. A thick puff of smoke rose as the hot steel sizzled in the cold oil. Wiggins flinched and stared as if he had never seen such a thing before.

Heating the next block, George went on, "After quenching, this stuff will test about sixty-five on a Rockwell hardness tester on the C-scale. That's too hard; it would chip if it got a sharp blow. We have to temper it some."

When the three pieces had cooled enough to be handled, he took them to the belt sander to shine one side to a bright silver color, then took them back to the torch. "You have to be even slower when you temper, or draw as a lot of people call it. Seems like the steel takes a while to organize itself inside. Bring it up slowly all around, and then you start to see the bright part turning tan color. It gets darker and mottled. When you see a little purple color show up, time to stop. Now that block will check out fifty-eight to sixty on the Rockwell tester, hard and tough both. Let it cool by itself."

When the other two pieces were finished, he said, "That's as good as anybody can do. Pick them up in the morning and get your fixture together. I'll check it and deliver it at noon at the latest. I just wanted you to see how we do things around here. We don't have the equipment, but we make do for our customers."

"I get one hour overtime," Wiggins said. "You told me to stay over."

George, slightly irritated, asked, "When are you going to bring in your personal tools?"

"I don't know. My brother-in-law has got them in hock. I do the best I can."

"Well, Mr. Wiggins, I'll ask you not to be talking union to the other hands here. If you have any complaints about wages or working conditions, bring them to me. Come in at eight tomorrow."

He wondered if he had been unduly bossy with his demonstration. The man had obviously learned something, if he was capable of learning.

His attitudes about the man were contradictory. He, himself, faced the problem of not having what they called "credentials," and believed that every man had to have a chance. But George was sixty-six years old now and shouldn't by trying to teach a bastard who resented learning. If Wiggins did not measure up, he was going out on his ear.

Dobbs called him that night at the house. He was in Ogallala, Nebraska, a place which had once been an important cowtown. He had again picked up the hot lead he had found in Dodge City, or at least believed it was the same old man.

"They say the man had white hair and could be nearly ninety, Mr. George Woodstock," Dobbs reported. "He wore a big hat and cowboy boots. I believe your father frequently wore a hat and boots, didn't he?"

"He didn't wear them for show. There's a good reason for wearing a big hat and boots when you're riding in mesquite brush out in the sun."

"Some of the descendants mentioned that he wore a cowboy hat and cowboy boots. This old gentleman registered two nights at a motel here, and he mentioned to a waitress that he once knew Wild Bill Hickok. Do you recall his mentioning such an acquaintance?"

"No," George told him. "I think it's ridiculous."

"Well, Mr. George Woodstock, we are talking about an old man who may have become childish, may imagine things, perhaps like a dream. I suppose your father was a cowboy, was he not?"

"He was one of the best cowhands in the country."

"I suppose he read a lot of western adventure stories, did he not?"

"No."

"He didn't read much?"

"He read a lot, but not western stories."

"Well, the purpose of this call is to ask you where your father might have gone from here. Deadwood? Helena? Where? Supposing that he is halfway lost and dreaming, looking for a romantic past, where would he go from Ogallala, Nebraska? Anything you can remember his saying, any slight hint, could be of importance."

"I can't think of anything."

"If you do, don't hesitate to call my headquarters, day or night. They will record your message for me. Well, I believe that we might be on a productive lead this time, Mr. George Woodstock. We can hope so."

"Yeah."

CHAPTER NINE

The Bone Man and the Hooker

As if he did not have enough on his mind with the shop and the mystery of Papa and Helen saying the oven timer was not right and had to be fixed, the bone man from Harvard—Overstreet—called. He was in town. George had a brief thought: at least the idiot had not asked to be picked up at the airport.

"Mr. Woodstock, I need to talk to you, but I'm ready to wait as long as necessary until it is convenient to you. I don't wish to disrupt your work or your social life or anything. What I wish to do is keep in touch until you have an hour or two. You could come to my hotel, or I could come wherever you ask."

"What did you want to talk about, Mr. Overstreet? Dr. Overstreet?"

"I believe I can assure you with the standards we have adopted that there will be no burden on the land owner. Then I would like to have the opportunity to explain the importance of the project we propose."

"We have this family problem, Professor Overstreet."

"Yes, Walter Woodstock explained. He is convinced that if you and the young ranch manager Johnny will agree, then there will be no difficulties. All I need at this time is an hour or so to talk to you. At your own convenience."

"Well, come on out to the house, Professor. I'm not agreeing to anything, except to listen."

"Now? Is now all right?"

"Soon as you get ready. Don't wait till after eight o'clock. I've got to get up early in the morning."

Overstreet was there in fifteen minutes. He was dressed in a khaki jacket, as if on a field trip, a kind of bubbling man, full of friendliness. He had a northern accent, putting "Rs" where they don't belong and leaving them off where they do belong. George liked him even though he fully intended to say No to this bone project. George had nothing but the cheapest canned beer he could buy, but the Professor accepted one gratefully.

"Now, Mr. Woodstock, ..."

"Call me George."

"Fine. Fine. Call me Oliver. I like your informality, George. First, let me read you a list of standards we jotted down for the protection of land owners. Number one: we will close any gate we open immediately after passing through. Number two: we will take care not to frighten or disturb any livestock. Number three: If we go to a pond or lake for water for drinking, cooking, or bathing, we will take care not to disturb any livestock that may be in the vicinity."

George said, interrupting, "You could change that pond or lake. We have tanks out there."

"Fine. Fine. That's interesting. Dr. Romer's notes mention something about that. It's Spanish derived, I guess. Tank it is. Number four: we will not shoot dove or quail or sage hens, nor any kind of game at all. And we will not fish. Number five: being aware of the danger of prairie fires, we will take due precautions, building any cook fire in our camp in a safe place and leaving at least one fire guard awake at every burning fire. Number six: we will not intrude into the activities of the land owner to ask for aid or information, except at his convenience. Number seven: in our preliminary survey, we will dig nowhere more than six inches deep except to remove a fossil which protrudes from the ground. Number eight: if we do any damage or cause any expense to the land owner, we will reimburse the land owner from our expense funds.

"Now, George, these are tentative. If you want to change some, fine. Fine. If you can think of something more, fine. Fine."

"They sound reasonable to me." He went and got them two more beers from the refrigerator. "But let me tell you some things about those bones out there. This is not a theory or science, but stuff I know personally. When you called before you mentioned Dead Cowbones Bluff. It's a cliff that drops off ninety or a hundred feet and below it is maybe four, five, six acres of red alkali, where nothing grows except maybe a few stunted cactus."

Overstreet said, "That's the place we're most interested in."

"Well, many a time back in the '30s I've helped drag a dead cow out there behind a wagon or just with a team. You put a rope on her horns or neck and on one back leg. You drag her close to the cliff, get the ropes off, and tumble her over.

"I didn't know why we did it until Papa explained it to me one time. Cows have diseases and you never know what one died from. You let a dead one lay around in the pasture, and she gets to working alive with the germs that killed her. Other stock may catch it. But cows don't come into that alkali flat, because there's no grass. They don't get within a hundred yards or more of the dead one. All that goes in there is maybe buzzards and coyotes."

"Wonderful, George. Fine. I think your Papa was wise. We did not have a good rationale for the many cow bones, and I'm sure your explanation will wind up in a scientific paper some day."

"Well, Professor . . . Oliver, what does this do to your dinosaur bones theory?"

"Okay, George. I don't want to get too technical, but

I'm glad you're interested. You can tell a lot about a bone from its size and shape, the way ligaments must have hooked on and such. The bones of domestic cattle at that site go back to around 1880. Then you go back past, say, 1700, and you find the bones of American bison, buffalo. Before they had the horse, the natives of the Great Plains used to lure and drive—maybe I should say stampede—the buffalo over a bluff, and that was one of their killing sites. The creatures would be dead or crippled, easy prey. We can tell the difference between domestic cattle bones and those of American bison.

"And we can tell something about their butchering methods by the marks of flint tools. It's interesting that the best buffalo marrow bones are missing; they carried them away to make soup.

"But, George, the site goes away back before the cliff was there. Past ten thousand years there are fossilized bones of the giant bison. Dr. Romer found a jaw tooth as big as your fist, undoubtedly from the biggest bovine creature that ever lived. Out in New Mexico, you know, they have found the same bones with a beautiful Folsom flint spear point embedded in them."

George interrupted. "Can I get you another beer?"

"Fine. Fine. George, you are the most hospitable host there ever was. Next time I come to see you I'll bring you a case of beer.

"I'm so enthused about the Dead Cowbones Bluff, George, that I run on and on. You see we are talking about millions of years. Mountains rose up and eroded away. Bones in a swamp were silted over for a million years and covered up a thousand feet, but in the next five million years that earth washed away from the wind and water, and the bones came into the sunlight. This happened again and again in northwest Texas. Creeks and rivers changed. What was once a bluff might be all cracked off and level a hundred thousand years later. In certain spots the various strata are very close together, or even mixed together.

"But the amazing thing is that we have exposed in the redbeds remnants of the early Permian days, around 250 million years ago. We have good skulls of eryops, one of the first animals ever to walk on land. Long before man, before any warm-blooded mammals, even before the famous dinosaurs. And it's possible that it's all there, within six acres, below Dead Cowbones Bluff. There is a fantastic history there, George, of animal life on earth."

George could not help liking the man, maybe on account of his enthusiasm. Anybody who enjoys beer can't be all bad.

Overstreet said, "Point me toward the bathroom, George. I have a little business there. You are undoubtedly the finest host in the world."

After another hour of praise of the redbeds and another six-pack of beer, Professor Oliver Overstreet went on. "Just let me make one point. We have five experts involved, and not one will receive a cent of profit or pay this summer if the project goes through. These are men who have credentials and have published. They will get the satisfaction of advancing science, and they will advance their careers. I don't deny that. They will have all expenses paid but will get nothing for their time and work.

"This foundation grant for the preliminary survey, George, only pays expenses to see whether a larger project is justified. We will map the site. We will shoot stadia for distance and elevation. That means . . . ."

Not to be intimidated George interrupted. "I was a pretty good surveyor. I know what you can do with a transit or alidade and a stadia rod."

"Fine. Fine. We would do a good survey of the immediate area. Take some pictures also. Take a couple of dozen soil samples, small samples. Analyze the layers, the strata, in the face of the bluff. We would collect bones only if they are obvious. This is a preliminary survey this summer, so that we will be able to make a full presentation to the foundation."

By the time Dr. Oliver Overstreet was ready to leave at midnight they had drunk nearly a case of beer, the man had given George a copy of the Standards to Protect the Landowners, and George had promised to call Johnny and say he thought it was okay.

Helen, padding around in a housecoat after the man left, had monitored some of the talk and she said she thought Overstreet was the nicest Yankee she ever heard.

Irma Abbott woke him up and got him out of bed at five-thirty the next morning, calling from Atlanta. "I know you go to work early, George," she said. "I wanted to catch you before you go to work."

It was hard to figure out exactly what his little sister wanted. She was worried about her youngest son, Larry, who had always been the black sheep of that family, nothing like his wonderful brother, Wilbur.

"He thinks he has some money coming, George. He has not worked in months, and he's running with low women and no telling who all."

"Well, I don't know what I can do, Irma. I have quite a few problems of my own."

"You can help straighten him out if he comes over there. He went to talk to Walter, and Walter actually had him thrown in jail. Can you imagine that? Larry won't listen to me. The last thing he said to me two weeks ago, along with some terrible curse words, was that he would see you and see if you would help him get his inheritance."

"Irma, I don't want any part of this. I'm busy."

"George, you've got to do what you can if he shows up. He's your own flesh and blood."

He ended the conversation as soon as he decently could without making any commitment.

Three days later he locked up the shop after the others had gone and went out to the Pontiac. A woman was there obviously waiting for him, leaning against the radiator grill. She was in her twenties, dressed in bright red slacks and a yellow blouse which was dirty. Her red tinted hair was not well kept. He could not help wondering if she was a prostitute.

"You Uncle George Woodstock?" she asked.

"Do I know you, young lady?"

"I'm Bonnie."

"Well, I'm afraid I'm too busy to talk to you."

"Your nephew Larry Abbott is in trouble and needs a little help. If you'll carry me out there I'll show you the way."

"What are you to Larry Abbott? Are you married or what?"

"We been like traveling together. In fact, Mister, I been supporting him. He's in bad trouble and needs a little consideration. Besides, he's got a proposition I think you'll be interested in if you know where your bread is buttered."

"I'm sorry. I have a dozen things to do and think about. Larry is sure old enough to take care of himself."

"Listen, old dude. You going to leave your own nephew out there living under a bridge? You ain't even willing to rap?"

He stared at her a minute. "Where is he?"

"Out where that farm road goes off from the interstate out there. I can show you."

He felt like a sucker and wondered if it could even be dangerous to go with this strange woman. She had something young about her face and talk, a look of dirty, stained innocence. He let her in the Pontiac and followed her directions down the streets. Evidently she had been walking around for a week or so in the area. On the narrow highway, a quarter mile off the interstate, she said, "Stop at that bridge."

The small creek which the old concrete bridge spanned was grown up with weeds and scrub willows. Someone, or several people, had dumped trash down the rough path beside the bridge abutment. He let Bonnie go well ahead. At the sound of tin cans being disturbed, a voice called out, "Who's that? I'm warning you! I'm armed!"

"It's me, Babe."

"Who's that dude? Bonnie, I told you good and well not to bring no tricks out here. This ain't no cat house."

"How in the hell am I going to get any johns interested when I can't even get a motel room and can't even buy any clean underclothes? I brought your damned sweet little Uncle George to see you."

The light was dim under the bridge. Larry, in his mid-thirties, with bushy black hair and beard, sat on the sloping bank, a large sharpened screwdriver in his hand—evidently what he meant when he said he was armed. Trash was mixed with the crushed down weeds. Under the middle of the bridge was a small pool of stagnant green water. George was thinking that here's what a hippie looks like when he's past that thirty mark. He thought he could catch the peculiar sweet smell of marijuana mixed in with toilet smells in the dank air.

"What's the trouble, Larry?"

"What the hell you mean, what's the trouble?"

"This young woman said you were in bad trouble."

"I ain't got no bread, man. My so-called mama and that idiot Uncle Walter won't give me any consideration at all. I come here to see if you got any decent sense. I don't want to come to your high-toney house. You know why? Because I don't want to make your high-toney wife and friends ashamed. I won't come to your house unless I have to. Just think about that a minute."

It sounded almost like a threat. George was wondering

whether maybe he should have brought along a tire iron or some kind of club. He stared at the younger man, waiting for an explanation.

"The old man Papa Franklin Woodstock happened to be my grandpa. He had about like a hundred square miles of land out there. I got something coming out of it. They all want to cut me out because they don't like my style. I want my share. You going to be like the others, or you going to admit there's a big ranch out there and part of it is mine?"

"There's nothing like a hundred square miles. Nobody knows anything about a will. I don't know what the law says. If Papa's dead."

"Hell, man, he's dead. He was about like a hundred years old. I've got a couple of propositions to put to you if you're smart."

George waited patiently.

"You got all that land out there and you can keep people out. Nobody would suspect a thing. It's a perfect set-up. You could grow the biggest crop of grass in the country out there in those creek bottoms. The law wouldn't ever catch on. There's a fortune in it for everybody, if the old fogies will go along. I could make us some contacts. You see where I'm coming from?"

"Yes, I do. We are already growing grass out there for cows to eat. You better get that idea out of your head. None of the old fogies will go along."

Bonnie said, "Tell him the other proposition, Babe. We got to get hold of some money."

"All right, here's one you can understand, Uncle. You have caught me in a tight. I took a course in how to write and asked for a job writing television stuff, but they laughed at me. I been learning to pick the guitar, but I can't get no gigs and had to hock it. Bonnie here could do good as an exotic dancer in a club, but she would need to buy some clothes. You got us in a tight.

"The fact is, Uncle. I'm willing to sell half my inheritance. You lay about a hundred bucks on me right now, then go and get some lawyer to make up the papers, and I'll sell you half of everything I got coming for five thousand. You can't beat that deal."

George had gotten enough of the whole scene, the trashy, weedy slopes, the rank smell, the strange conversation. "Larry, I've got to go. I don't think you have any inheritance coming by a will or by law, and wouldn't touch your proposition if you did. Anyway, I've got plenty of problems of my own. I've got thirty some-odd bucks here . . . ."

He found thirty-seven dollars in his billfold and thrust it into the hand of the bearded young man. "Here. Call your mother. Hell, tell her you've been born again."

Bonnie giggled.

George started back up the poor trail, but paused to say, "Don't come to my house or my shop. I'll call the cops if you do."

About all he could think of was to get home, get his shoes off, prop his feet up, and have a beer.

CHAPTER TEN

Irma and Walter

IRMA called from Atlanta. George was at home in the middle of dressing for a crippled-children's function Helen had persuaded him to go to, where somehow they were raising money for a good cause.

"George," Irma pleaded, "we've got to do something. Walter just wants to find Papa dead so he can take charge and he's trying his best right now."

"What's Walter done?"

"He wants to hold a meeting with you and Clarence and me and Clara in July to get the lawyers to declare Papa dead, because Papa would be missing three months in July."

"Well, I don't think lawyers can do that."

"You know what I mean, George. Lawyers can get the courts to do anything if somebody like Walter is prodding them and we don't object and stop them. He says July, and Wilbur has a crusade for three weeks in July in the State of Indiana. It's all set with the local ministers, and Wilbur is the main evangelist, and I think Walter just said July on purpose so I can't be at the meeting."

"Well, do you have to be at the crusade, Irma?"

"I certainly do. I am going to stand behind Wilbur and his important work every way I can. In spite of what Walter might say, I think that's what Papa would want. We talked about this before and I think you saw that Papa was a born-again Christian, and you know he would want us to spread the gospel. George, that Walter thinks he's such a big shot he doesn't want to think about anybody else, and he's going to try to turn you and Clara and Clarence against me so he can have his way."

George was thinking that she wanted to have her way as much as Walter did, and both of them were going to have to give way sooner or later. Yet he felt the need to keep the whole matter as peaceful as possible.

"Look, Sis, I'm sure that any meeting we have will be so that you can be present. I'll guarantee it."

"Then you'll support our plan for a religious retreat and the Noah's Ark? You'll help explain to Clara and Clarence what Papa would have wanted, so we can block Walter? I knew you would, George."

"No. I didn't say that. Look, Sis, we all have different ideas, but we have to get along together. Things will work out."

"Tell me," she said, "why Walter got so much satisfaction when I made a mistake. That detective he hired to chase around wanted a picture of Papa, so I gave him one, but it turned out to be a picture of Papa's brother Milt that died twenty years ago. I confessed that I made a mistake when I remembered it. But Walter made a big deal out of it, like I was crazy or something."

She want on ranting, repeating herself. George was wondering whether he should mention Larry, maybe even ask whether Larry had recently been born again. She was not proud of that son. Maybe it would cool her down to discuss the black sheep. He remembered her saying ten years ago: Train up a child in the way he should go, and when he is old he will not depart from it. She had done the training up.

But he did not have time to play games. Helen was standing waiting. "Look, Sis, there will not be any meeting unless all five of us can be there. I'll guarantee it. I have to go. Thanks for calling."

They were supposed to bring something to drink to the

function. Helen had a bottle of pink wine, so George got a six-pack of beer out of the refrigerator. She asked him to put on a tie and jacket and to please put ten or twenty dollars in a collection box they would have handy.

The function, or party, in a big old run-down house with a big patio, turned out to be better than he expected. It seemed to be mostly women, some nearly seventy, who had brought their husbands, and none of them had a snooty air about them.

Four guys brought their guitar and mandolin and banjo and fiddle. And they played. They called themselves the "Barnyard Boys" and sang through their nose and tried to sound like Bill Monroe. They sang "Irene, Goodnight," "Truck Driver's Blues," "Corina, Corina," "Frankie and Johnny," "Going Down the Road Feeling Bad," "Power in the Blood," "Wreck of the Old Ninety-Seven," the "Ballad of Jessee James," and other songs. And fiddle breakdowns without the words: "Ragtime Annie," "Way Down Yonder," "Rubber Dolly," and "Soldier's Joy."

It was the only party he had really liked for years. He took off his tie and stuffed it in his coat pocket. Several of the men and women could be seen tapping their toes to the rhythm.

The fiddle player got drunk about midnight, and everyone went home.

Walter called from New York two days later at exactly one minute after nine in the morning. He knew the time difference between East Coast and Central Standard and he believed that any good executive was sitting at his desk at nine and had ordered a cup of coffee from his secretary. Actually George had been at the shop three hours and was trying to figure up some bids.

After a few exchanges of how's everything going?

George said, "Irma is kind of put out with you about the meeting. She says she can't make it."

"George, Irma is looking for something to complain about. Clara is a dingbat, as all of us agree, but Irma is crazy. Let's face it; she's crazy. She gets these passionate ideas and wants to control everything and will not listen to reason. There is not one whit of problem about whether she can make it. We will have the meeting when all of us can make it. I called her yesterday, and she admitted that she has nothing scheduled for August fifteenth. So that's the date. She has no excuse. If she is interested in her own father and his property, she will appear at the meeting. That is, if you and Clarence agree to the date. Clara agrees."

"Well, Walter, the only thing that bothers me is what the meeting is for. It seems like from what Irma said we're giving up on Papa. That we're going to give up on him and settle everything and do something with his ranch."

"No, George, no. Our private investigator is headed for Montana now on what may prove to be a hot lead. We will stay right on top of the search. The point, however, is that we cannot get five busy people together for an important meeting unless we plan well ahead of time. Within the next two weeks I have three important dates here in the city, one conference in Boston, and a convention in Philadelphia. You are a businessman, and you know you cannot turn loose whenever you wish unless you schedule ahead of time."

He thought the older brother sounded a little patronizing, even though it made sense. He said, "Then you think on August the fifteenth we should hold a meeting and see if we can get Papa declared dead?"

"George, I think on August the fifteenth we should get together and try to agree on some order and authority. Who got the private investigator? Me. Who is arranging for a firm of accountants to look into the ranch affairs and make a report? Me. Irma does very well when it comes to complaining or inventing harebrained schemes, but when it comes to *doing* something, she does not do worth a damn.

"And, George, I've had long telephone conversations with two different MDs out there. They had examined and treated Papa and knew his records. One said he had estimated a year ago that Papa had only six months to live; the other had said the same thing about nine months ago. This is not some exact prognosis, but an honest opinion of dependable old country doctors. They based it on his heart and lungs and liver and digestive system.

"I told them that he is very tough, and they agreed, but they said he is also very tired and wants to rest. They said he might go out in some dramatic way and that he did not want to be cared for hand and foot by a nursemaid. I agreed with them."

"Well, do you believe this detective Dobbs has any chance of finding him?"

"I don't know. All these do-nothings say Papa's got to be somewhere. One thing about Papa's being on the ranch. I'll say this for Johnny: nobody on the whole wide earth knows the ranch like that kid."

George cut off the call by agreeing that he would definitely be at the meeting on August the fifteenth. Then he got back to work.

An idea briefly crossed his mind: one person on the whole wide earth might know the ranch better than Johnny. But the idea was lost when Bob Fowler came in with a drill jig ready to deliver to the customer.

It seemed that the August meeting was working up to be a free-for-all unless Walter or Irma gave way, which they would not do easily. They would have to compromise, split things up or something. George determined to have his say at the meeting and to favor some kind of split which would let him take out the hundred thousand Papa had promised for the machine shop. It was kind of shameful to be assertive, demanding about what was to be done with the inheritance; he had felt that about Walter and Irma's ideas. But maybe, if they had found nothing by the middle of August, when Papa had been missing four months, it would be different.

He knew that he was held up in a certain way because they had all gone to college. Even Clara had two years of junior college. Irma had a degree in social science or something. Clarence had a PhD in literature. And Walter had his MBA from a big-shot school. He had nothing. But he honestly did not believe that any of them could do what he had done in surveying, aerial navigation, or toolmaking.

Did any of the four ever look at a telephone line he had run over Douglas Pass near the Colorado-Utah line—that ran straight as a string up and down the mountains and rough country for miles and miles? Did any of the four ever find the radio compass out of whack, all radio communication out because of a gas leak, and grab at the rare chance of a noon fix on the sun, plotting the actual sub point of the sun on the chart, swinging the arcs to make lines of position, and come straight in to the airport at Hilo? Did any of the four ever hold in his hand an inspection gauge of hardened steel he had made to accurately check rock drilling bits, with various angles and a hole for a tooling ball, all ground and lapped to within two tenths of a thousandth of an inch?

Sometimes he felt intimidated by intellectuals, wondering what they knew that he did not, but at other times he felt contempt for them, even pity.

The Wiggins fellow would not let the idea of a union alone. George caught him in a free moment and asked, "What is all this talk about a union?"

"A labor union, Mr. Woodstock. I know you people

down here in this part of the country must have heard of such a thing." Wiggins was grinning as if a grin would make an insult okay. "So the employees can bargain collectively."

"In a shop this size with five employees?"

"Why, we need protection much as anybody."

"Nobody needs protection here or needs to bargain if they can do the work. I need good hands and I'll pay them if they will work where I can make a small profit on what they do. The other employees here are not going to pay any attention to you. I suggest that you shut up about a union."

"It's illegal to threaten me because I believe in unions."

"Well, then I'll ask you not to stand around talking about it when you're supposed to be working. And I'll ask you when you mean to bring in your tools, the basic tools every toolmaker and machinist is supposed to have."

"Hell, Woodstock, I can't help it if I had bad luck and ain't got no tools." The man mumbled something about a "Labor Board" and went back to work.

That afternoon the steel company delivered a load of heavy ten-inch pipe, to be used in a contract for six welded structures. Wiggins said that he could not do arc welding, but he was good with a cutting torch. George assigned him the job of cutting the material to length. Though the pipe was heavy, it was only a one-man job to roll the sections around with a crowbar and roll the pieces through the wide back door onto the concrete floor of the shop.

Twenty four of the pieces had to be cut with a curve in the end so as to form a ninety detree T-joint when butted and welded against another pipe of the same size. To cut the curve it was necessary to wrap a pattern of brown paper, which George had in his files, around the pipe at the right place, tape it down, and mark around the edge with a piece of soapstone. Then take the pattern off and follow the mark with the cutting torch. The cut did not need to be extremely accurate. A little grinding with a body sander to take off the tops of any high places, and any gaps would be filled in with the welding bead later.

The torch stayed lit all the time and only did its cutting when the oxygen lever was gripped. Wiggins marked the first curve, took off the pattern, and laid it aside. He did the cutting with a great sputter of white and red hot steel, separated the scrap end, raised his dark goggles, laid the torch aside, still burning, and proceeded to light up a cigarette. The brown paper pattern blazed up.

Fowler was stomping out the paper by the time George got there, but the pattern was ruined.

George said, "That's the only pattern I've got for ten-inch pipe. Mr. Wiggins, you are through. We can't afford to have you around."

The man was grinning that insolent grin. "What the hell's the problem? Have the engineers give us another pattern."

"There are no engineers, unless I want to pay them a big fee."

"Well, you could have cut out a new pattern from the old one and had an extra. It ain't my fault."

"Can you understand anything, man? You are fired. Come to the office and I'll write out your check. Take off my goggles."

"I'll take it to the Labor Board."

"You do just that. If there is such a thing as a Labor Board, tell them to check with the other employees here and see if they think you are qualified to do the work you hired on to do."

When he had got rid of the man, it was five o'clock. He told Fowler that he would have a new pattern by morning.

He sat for a while at his desk with a yellow ruled pad, sketching a side view of a cylinder with a half circle of the same diameter cut out of the end, and sketching an end view of the same cylinder, then a rough view of the double curve of the flat pattern. He moved hypothetical figures from one view to the other. It was obvious that the length of the pattern should be Pi times the OD, or 31.416 inches for a ten-inch pipe. What he had to do was plot points, say a half inch apart, from the ends and the straight side of the pattern.

Just before dark he made a quick trip to the 7-11 store to get a six pack of beer to reward himself for working at night. If it did not sharpen his mind, at least it reduced the frustration.

One thing—now he had a decent calculator. Many a time, trying to figure such a problem he had found it necessary to use log-trig functions; now he could use simple trig functions. When he finally saw the way to get the square coordinates for the points, he remembered a happy fact he had figured out years before: you don't need to figure out but a fourth of the points. There were two curves just the same, and they were each symmetrical so that the plus figure on one side were just minus figures on the other.

He taped a piece of good drafting paper onto the drafting table and began to plot. A tape measure would have been close enough, but he did it carefully with his long Lufkin scale and dividers and trammels. Luckily he found a piece of heavy wrapping paper to which he transferred his curve points by pricking through the drafting paper with a needlepoint scribe. He cut out, the new pattern with a pair of sheet metal shears and labeled it "T-joint, ten inch."

He had called Helen at eight o'clock to say he would be late. She called the shop just before midnight.

"George, is everything all right?"

"Sure. I'm about finished."

"You don't need some help, do you? Are you sweeping the shop or something I could do? You're not hurt, are you?"

"No, Helen. I'll be right home. I just had to get this problem figured out before the hands come in tomorrow."

The woman needed to get a job was what she needed. Not that she spent too much money, but she just didn't have anything hard to do that she could take pride in. Once he had asked her to come work in the shop and learn to use a drill press, but she had turned down the offer. Now she had taken up needlework for a pastime, mostly doing doll dresses for the Girl Scouts and knitted house shoes for the orphans' home.

George had thought about it in the years after turning sixty. There are things to do in the years after you marry, like raise kids, make a living, get a decent, comfortable house to live in. Then, when those things are done, you may not have much in common. She had never understood his work, the beauty of an accurate, machined piece of steel, parts that fit right and do what they are supposed to do, machinery and devices that work right and hold up and keep on working right.

CHAPTER ELEVEN

The Snows of Yesteryear

CLARENCE called from California. Classes were out and he was off till September, he said, and he was feeling guilty because he had not helped any in the search or in taking care of Papa's affairs. He had talked several times on the phone to Walter and Clara and Irma. He thought he should go out to the ranch and at least see whether there was anything he could do.

"I know you're busy, George," he said. "You don't get a summer vacation. But I wondered whether you would like to run out there for a day or two. I'd like to talk to you anyway about these schemes of Walter and Irma."

George realized that his younger brother knew that he had picked up both Walter and Irma and hauled them to west Texas. It looked like now that he ought to do the same for Clarence. In fact, he thought that Clarence was probably the easiest of his kin to get along with.

He agreed to pick his brother up on Thursday, but explained the conditions: He did not want to find a parking place in that confusion, but wanted to be called when the flight arrived and would pick him up in front of whatever airline terminal he came in on.

"Be great to see you, George," Clarence said. "Frank wants to come with me. Okay? He's in geology here at the university."

"Okay."

There were things to do, instructions to give, if he was going to be away from the shop. He started to refuse to make a bid on a job, but Fowler thought he could handle it all right, so George went ahead, telling Fowler to work himself and the others all the overtime they had to. George figured he would be gone two days.

Clarence was waiting at the right place. He got in the front seat, and his son Frank got in the back seat with the bags. George realized that it really was good to see them.

Clarence was an easygoing man of sixty-four, a little overweight, with steel-gray hair and a big bald spot. He had a noticeable scar on his cheek. A parachutist, he had jumped behind German lines in France on D-day, 1944. He had got a purple heart for the scar, but would not talk about the details; Walter had said that he probably came down in a tree. Funny, how Clarence had been a private "in the rear ranks" as he always put it and had jumped right into the middle of the war, while Walter, who was a captain, worked in some kind of logistics office in Washington.

Frank, in his late thirties, was a carbon copy of his father, without the bald head and the scar. He let the older men do the talking.

George said, "What do you think about all this mixmaster freeway stuff in Fort Worth of all places? You have to be a genius to read the highway signs."

Clarence chuckled. "It doesn't exactly fit our image of Cowtown. But, say, when did you last drive around LA?"

"In the '60s. Maybe twenty years ago we were out there."

"It's ridiculous now, George. If you get caught in the rush hour, you may as well give up, and the rush hour is all day and half the night. I have an idea for a short story I'm going to write. Based on the Flying Dutchman myth, the old ship that sails forever. This family from Arkansas is driving the LA freeways in an old rattletrap. They go around and around. Every time they find a turn to escape, they are in the wrong lane, so they go on forever."

"How do they get gas?"

"You're too practical, George."

When they were lined out on the straight highway west, Clarence said, "George, I wanted Frank to come along and he wanted to come along because we want to discuss a certain subject. The first consideration right now is to find Papa, but if we do I suspect that Walter will want a court to appoint him the legal guardian of Papa's person and property. In any case, it appears that something may be done about the ranch by August the fifteenth."

George said, "I'm not real happy about Walter's plans or Irma's."

"Neither am I. What we want to discuss is oil. This is not a proposal or a proposition. It is only a consideration. First, as I recall, the exploration and production people get seven-eighths; the land owner or owner of the mineral rights gets one-eighth. It is the people in the oil business who make the money. It would be possible for the land owners to handle the whole thing if they understood what they were doing. As I recall, Papa had as many as six producing wells at one time or another on the place. Do I remember right?"

"Probably more than that. You know that old cable and junk and rod lines we used to find out past Plum Creek? There must have been two or three wells pumping over there about the time we were born. But I think the most Papa ever saw was maybe fifty bucks a month at the most."

"Right, George. Well, a couple of factors to be considered. First, that oil was selling for a dollar a barrel or less. Twenty dollars a barrel is a different ball game, as they say. Second, all that production was shut down because they found more production in Louisiana, in California, overseas at various locations. It remains true that petroleum, the most convenient fossil fuel, is in finite supply, especially with the developing countries beginning to industrialize. Oil will play out. Meanwhile, the price of crude will rise to compete with coal, oil-shale, atomic energy, and other alternates. The price will rise within ten years.

"Well, that's what we wanted to consider, George. As you know, Frank began his education in geology at the school in Wichita Falls, so he knows something of the geological formations in northwest Texas. We have talked about this a few times, and we agree that there will not be any hard-sell, as they say."

George put in, "Well, suppose you take fifty a month at a dollar a barrel and make that thirty a barrel; that's only fifteen hundred a month. Not exactly riches."

"And suppose, George, you take eight-eighths instead of one-eighth. That's twelve thousand a month. Still not riches. But I want Frank to explain a few possibilities."

"Well, Uncle George, all that oil was shallow stuff. They went down hundreds of feet instead of thousands. Most of the holes were put down with cable tools, spudders instead of rotary rigs. There is a possibility, only a possibility, that there are deeper pools. The strata are very unpredictable.

"But, Uncle George, they could hit a producing well and still not pump it. They plugged some producing wells. They pumped with gasoline engines instead of electric motors. That meant they had to have an engine at each well or a rod line running out to it. Very inefficient. It took a man to watch the gasoline engines, and his wages might eat up the production.

"Then they usually had a storage tank at each well, and a tank truck had to come out across the prairie to gather in the crude. Very inefficient. On top of all that, their secondary recovery methods were not as well developed as they are today. We can get more oil out of a hole than we once could."

Clarence said, "Frank is not an oil geologist, but he

knows a lot about it. What do you think about these ideas, George?"

"Well, they were shooting wells with nitroglycerin back in the '30s. And they were treating them with acid. Remember that big wooden tank over on the railroad? Full of muriatic acid, I think it was. We used to find some spilled acid over there and throw rocks in it to watch it bubble."

"I remember that, George. But, of course, the point is that secondary methods are better now. I don't know anything about it, but we are talking about fifty years of development in oil technology. I imagine that includes seismograph interpretation as well as other things."

After a short silence, waiting for more comments by the older men, Frank went on. "If Papa's offspring formed an exploration and production company, it would be a good thing to keep it quiet at first. The first thing to do would be to gather as much information as possible, like well logs, records of production. Every kind of information. Most of those wells were drilled by independent producers, and if they kept a drilling log, they may have thrown it away if they got a dry hole. In fact, some of them may have pulled out and moved the rig when they were fifty feet from oil, because they hit a hard rock strata. There are records, even from seismographic crews, shooting in shallow holes and recording the return waves. Information for fifty miles around the ranch would be pertinent.

"But, Uncle George, this record searching and copying would have to be secret. Some of the land in northwest Texas has been sold two or three times. A lot of those who owned the land in the '20s kept the mineral rights when they sold it. There are people who own one-thirty-second of the mineral rights in a quarter section, and they dream that they might get rich some day from it. If an oil exploration and production company is formed by Papa's descendants, they need to get the information first. Then, get leases on any favorable land adjoining. The ranch is 7,680 acres and would make a good base, but there is no point in proving the potential for other people on adjoining land."

George, thinking about the secrecy and this business called "strata," got a sudden idea about the bone man, Overstreet. He asked Frank, "What about this bare land, just patches, we used to call alkali flats?"

"That's what the paleontologists call the redbeds, Uncle George. Like out there under Dead Cowbones Bluff. It's pretty deep in places and breaks out on the surface in others. Very old stuff. What's under them? Who knows? It's sure not the lava of the earth's core."

"Do you all know about this Harvard bunch? They couldn't be after information about oil, could they?"

Both Frank and Clarence laughed. Clarence said, "No, George, they are after bones. The Harvard expedition has no selfish interest. They only want to advance science. Well, one or another of the men may want to make full professor or professor emeritus. But oil to them is a phenomenon, a variety of fossil plants and animals gone bad, not a way to make money. They could not care less."

George asked, "Does Frank want to be president or something of this new oil company?"

"No, Uncle George. No. I believe it's up to the five immediate descendants as to what they want to do with the ranch. We think they ought to consider the oil possibilities. A pretty good cattle operation could be continued right along with an oil exploration and production company. If such a company is formed, and they ask me to work for it, I'll consider it carefully. I'm not an expert, but I'm aware of the possibilities of new methods in oil exploration such as near surface magnetic anomalies and airborne gravity exploration. Also new secondary and tertiary recovery methods such as thermal, chemical, and carbon dioxide flooding."

George was thinking that it was time to enter his own claim, at least to this brother and nephew. He said, "I have a thing that's been on my mind. I'll mention it to you all, but ask you not to bring it up to anybody else. Okay?"

"Okay, George."

"Well, Papa told me he would invest a hundred thousand bucks in my shop. He said as soon as I was ready. He liked my ideas about a tooling shop, I guess because the owners would work, and Papa was always his own best hand on the ranch. Then, too, we agreed that a big operation is not always the most efficient. There is a best size, where you have the equipment and everything you need, but the top bosses know what's going on. You don't have a long string of authority where you get orders mixed up and changed. I've proved the idea over and over by subcontracting work from big outfits and saved them money and made money myself too. And Papa said he had proved it by making more money per acre than bigger outfits, even ones using helicopters and squeeze chutes and all that, just by being in the middle of it himself.

"Anyway, Clarence, he told me that he would come up with a hundred thousand for machinery whenever I said. It would be an investment or a loan, not a gift. I was waiting to hire some hands and check them out. Now, I don't have any witness that he made the promise."

"You don't need any witness, George. Your word is certainly good to me at least, and to Clara. There may be some trouble with Walt and little Irma because they have their schemes. But there should be some way, some division, perhaps some way for you to take out that much money. Maybe some assets could be disposed of. I am glad you mentioned the promise, for we need to know what we face, and some decision may need to be made by August the fifteenth. There is no question in my mind that your share of the estate is more than the amount you mention."

When they were only thirty minutes from the town of

Woodstock, Clarence brought up a new subject. "One thing Frank and I have talked about is the problem of lawyers. I don't doubt that Walter will employ a law firm if he does not already have one on retainer. As long as they work for him, that's one situation; if we commit ourselves so that they are empowered to settle the estate, that's another situation. We might find that a lawyer is legally able to act for us, but in fact is working for Walter. George, are you familiar with *Bleak House,* by Charles Dickens?"

"I don't think so."

"Well, at the beginning of the novel there is an old estate to settle, Jarndyce versus Jarndyce. There is a long story, five or six hundred pages about the poor people who might be heirs and, indeed, might be wealthy if they inherited. Then at the end of the book the case is finally settled. It is definitely settled. The lawyers have eaten up the entire estate with a truck load of paperwork and their resulting fees; therefore, there is nothing left to do. The case has gone away."

They all laughed.

At the ranch Izzy hugged and exclaimed over Clarence and Frank as if they were long-lost brothers. She insisted on feeding them a late lunch and apologized for only having light bread from the grocery store. There would be home-baked bread for supper; she assured them that it had risen twice and was ready for the oven.

Clarence went out horseback with Johnny to search Plum Creek again. George and Frank prowled around the barns and pens and the flourishing garden. George called Clara and she said she would get Annie and come to supper to see her brother and nephew. When Clarence unsaddled at dusk he rubbed his bottom and revealed that he had spent the afternoon trying to keep Homer from falling off of Old Baldy, or trying to get him back on. They had found no trace of Papa.

Clarence sat in an overstuffed chair in the library after supper, tired and relaxed. He said he had not worked so hard physically in forty years, nor had such a good supper. "Nostalgia," he said. "Doesn't it bring back the old days, George? Fifty years ago and more."

"Yeah."

"Remember riding horseback to school? Old Easter? And Fanny? And Billy Bones?"

"Yeah, and all of us boys wanted to ride Easter, because the word was that he wouldn't carry double. He would kick-up when another kid tried to get on. So the boys on that old mare and Billy Bones had to carry a sister."

"Remember when Easter dumped you off on a rattlesnake over in prairie dog town?"

"Yeah, he shied sideways right on top of that booger. I went straight down and my hand actually touched that damned snake. He was trying to coil up, and I did some fast rolling to get away."

"And when we caught Easter he was headed home. We could outrun him riding double because he had to hold his head to the side to keep from stepping on the reins."

"Walter wasn't double when you all caught Easter. He pushed Clara off. She was behind the saddle on Billy Bones, and Walter just pushed her off. She claimed he tore her bloomers and made her fall in some stickers."

"Yeah. Remember when we were trapping and had some traps on the way to school. We caught a skunk, and Walter got it on him. I think he was in high school. Anyway, the principal made him stand outside. Mother couldn't wash the smell out, and she made him bury his clothes."

"Say, maybe that's a way we could blackmail Walter. We could threaten to tell some of his big business friends about the skunk deal."

"Good idea, George."

"I'll tell you one thing about Walter I remember. You know we used to sell skins to old Wiley at the feed store, and he would complain about every one, so we wouldn't want a big price. One time we took in five or six possum and skunk hides, all stretched and cured out, and Wiley would jerk a little hair out of each skin and say it was shedding. This one possum hide had a small hole, and he said, 'This one's no good; you boys need to learn to skin a varmint without cutting it all up.' And he dropped it in the trash box. Walter dug it out and said he'd just take it home, so Wiley said he guessed he'd give a quarter for it after all."

"Yeah," Clarence said. "And then he wouldn't give us our share of the quarter, because he said he earned it himself by taking a worthless fur out of the trash."

"Remember when us three boys played hookey on April Fool's Day and went exploring, and Irma told Papa on us?"

"Yeah. Mother thought we should have a whipping, but Papa said one time on April the first was all right. But don't ever do it again."

"You know, Clarence, Mother was always sick, and we didn't realize it."

"I've thought about that. In a way it is strange how little people know about their parents. How they felt. What they wanted. How they looked at the world. What they intended. It is even more obscure when you go back to earlier generations. We know nearly nothing about our grandparents."

"I reckon it goes on and on," George said. "How many people today understand how it was to ride horseback to school? If they didn't grow up in a place like this and during the depression, they don't know. Making soap. Killing hogs. Canning stuff."

"Yeah, our offspring will not understand."

Clarence stood up. "In regard to the matter of understanding Papa, did you ever read that verse he wrote? A copy is here somewhere, stuck in a book."

"I don't guess so."

"It's stuck in a book, some translation of one of the Greek playwrights. Sophocles? Aeschuylus?" He was browsing along the shelves. "Wait, here it is. Yes, it's still here." He took out a piece of paper and unfolded it.

"Did Papa write it?"

"It's in his handwriting. I asked him and he just chuckled."

"Do you think he wrote it?"

"I believe he did. I know a good bit of poetry, from the past and modern things. I cannot place this anywhere."

In a moment Clarence began to read, not declaiming, but as if he were standing in front of a class.

I see the dice are in my hand again.
These fools around the blanket
Toss my money in to fade my money.
My point is always four,
And I am central figure on this floor of sin.

Into the prim white cubes I hotly blow,
Seducing virgin dice that do not know the lust of game,
And cry to them,
As Roman soldiers cried two thousand years ago.

You have but six and thirty ways to fall they say,
But I sustain a shaking faith they may be wrong.
Who, after all, can tell
What magic number you might make some day?

Oh, Spirit! Come forth one time from Kokimo!
He hears his Papa's orders. Now!
I'll have you, Joe,
If neither comrade fool around the blanket,
Nor time's sharp hand reach down to catch my throw.

George noticed that Homer was standing in the door of the library, listening. Clarence stood with eyebrows slightly raised as if waiting for a reaction.

George asked, "Is it a good poem? You're a professor of literature."

"I think it is. It is old-fashioned in a way. Peculiar rhyme scheme. I would say it is good verse. It makes one think." Clarence laughed. "I showed it to Irma one time, and she insisted that Papa did not write it. She said it is about playing dice and Papa certainly never played dice and did not know anything about it.

"I suggested that maybe he learned to shoot craps in the army. She insisted that Papa was never in the army. She remembered very well; he was right here on the ranch, doing his patriotic duty, raising meat for the boys overseas.

"I suggested that there was a war before we were born and reminded her that Papa had a trunk containing a gas mask, a victory medal, a variety of French coins, and a picture of himself standing by a big artillery piece.

"She admitted that he may have been in the army in 1918, but said he certainly did not play dice and would not have written a poem about gambling. I had to surrender in order to keep from getting a further lecture."

Homer had come into the room. He tried to tell them something, then went to the far end of the shelves, near the bottom, searched a minute, then opened a book, and took out a folded paper. He handed it to Clarence and said, "Papa."

The professor said, "It's his handwriting," then he read:

I started up at half past three
And stared at the face of Eternity.
Her hair was wild; her brow was wide,
Like silent snow on the mountainside.
Thank God! her lips were tender red.
She marked my awe, smiled, and said,
"Fine young fellow, have no fear.
I visit each man in his eightieth year.
But you have several yet to live,
And I have presents yet to give."

George saw that Annie, in her pajamas, was standing in the doorway, listening, and he wondered if he and Clarence were talking too loud. He decided they were not; the youngsters were just curious.

The two brothers talked about how few who had known Papa would have guessed that he tried to write poetry. Many of the ranchers and cowhands he had been around would have said: "What the hell is poetry? Old Frank sure don't know nothing about it."

Clarence got a sudden idea. "Say, if Papa wrote a will, would he have stuck it in one of these books? A handwritten will is legal. A will could be hidden anywhere on this ranch. We ought to think about it."

Equally as sudden, Annie pleaded, "No! It's a secret!"

They stared at her and laughed a little.

Clara came in her baggy gray nightgown and picked up the child, a good load for her aging arms and back. "It's all right, sweetheart. Come on. Back to bed."

"But, Grandmother! It's a true secret!"

"It will be all right, sweetheart. Come on, Homer honey, time to hit the hay." She smiled at the two men and added, "These old men may talk all night." She took the youngsters.

In a minute Clarence asked, "What was that all about?"

"Well, she says that Papa willed her the jackrabbits and the hawks and all the flowers. Probably the prairie dogs and coyotes and crawdads too. The whole shooting match."

Clarence chuckled wryly. "Old men get that way about little kids. Was it Stevenson or Dickens who gave his birthday to a little girl?"

They went out to the Pontiac, where George had a case of beer in the trunk, and brought out two six-packs. Clarence agreed that beer has more taste to it when it's warm. They had both learned to drink warm beer in the service in the early '40s.

They remembered certain teachers they had loved or

hated more than half a century ago, kids they had known, fights they had been in. They remembered chores, shucking corn for the hogs and a team, chopping wood before Papa got the chain saw and long before he put in butane gas, hauling manure from the barns and chicken houses to put on the garden and orchard. They remembered milking half-tame range cows that had too much milk for their calves and how the barn cats would come around and beg, and how they loved to have milk squirted in their faces. How George had invented the idea of inserting a small feather quill into the cow's teat and the milk would drain out without squeezing, an idea which probably ruined the cow's plumbing. They remembered hunting the hidden nests of guineas and turkeys. They remembered riding miles with axes in the coldest weather to help chop drinking holes in the tanks for the stock.

They remembered the tree house down in the old giant live oak, how they had carried and dragged boards from the Old Place to make a ladder and a clubhouse ten feet above the ground. How they had gathered rusty nails and straightened them, most of them square nails probably made by a blacksmith. How George had invented a light made out of a bottle full of coal oil with a piece of rope pushed into it for a wick. How Clara and little Irma had sneaked into the tree house and lighted the lamp, and Irma had turned it over and nearly burned the tree down.

After midnight they got the other two six-packs out of the trunk of the Pontiac. A couple of hours later Clarence developed a new idea.

"George, you know there is an obscure novelist named Benjamin Capp or something like that. They use his writings in literature courses. I read one of his novels in which an old Indian throws himself away. It is a poignant account, and believable. The point is that the old man knows that he is of no use to himself or anyone else and, in fact, is somewhat of a burden. He is forgetful and not productive, and he knows they care for him out of sentimentality. He is proud and does not want the family to take care of his private physical needs as if he were a baby. He wants to be the final arbiter of his destiny on the Earth Mother. Therefore, he throws himself away.

"Who can read the mind of an old man like that, George? Did Papa come to thinking in that vein? That silly private investigator told me on the phone that Papa maybe went out to New Mexico to make a mummy out of himself in a dry cave. If Papa decided to throw himself away, I believe he would make a compact with someone he trusted to lay him to rest out there in the Woodstock Cemetery, where Mother is, and his own father and brother."

George said, "We could check that. Not too many burials out there. Without a marker or anything we could still see the dirt disturbed. It hasn't rained hardly at all here this spring."

They agreed to go to the cemetery and look tomorrow, or rather today. Good thing there were three bathrooms in the house, after all that beer. They both got to sleep before dawn.

CHAPTER TWELVE

Cloudy in the West

GEORGE had risen before six o'clock in the morning so long that he could not sleep even though he knew he was sleepy. Clarence seemed to be settled in for peaceful snoring until around noon.

Johnny and Izzy were bustling about. Johnny came in with two foaming buckets of milk. Izzy already had the washing machines going out on the screened porch.

Johnny asked, "Mother, are you doing that laundry for Slim's family again?"

"*Quien sabe*?" she said, smiling.

"Why? That's not part of the deal with Slim and Buck. You give them butter and peaches and all kinds of things. Now you've got them bringing their laundry over here. Why do you want to slave for them?"

She laughed. "Is it slaving to throw dirty clothes in a hole in a machine? With two automatic washers and two automatic dryers and all the hot water I want, I have to do something."

"You're spoiling them." He was halfway laughing too.

"Yes, you big stingy. Who does welding for them, and who pays them for a whole day when they only work four or five hours? And you went over there twice last winter to help them kill hogs."

"Well, be sure and hang them on hangers and fold them nice, Mother. You may want to iron some too."

"*Sí*! What's the world coming to when little boys scold their mothers?"

She said to George, "The coffee's ready. How about some nice sausage and eggs and toast? Or some pancakes? We have sorghum or some plum jam."

He said, "Believe I'll wait till Clarence gets up, Izzy. We stayed up late."

She laughed. "You stayed up all night. It's good to see brothers get along so fine."

Johnny said, "Looks like we might get some rain. Sure hope so. We can use it."

Outside, George saw that the early sun was hidden by thin clouds, but in the west the sky was mottled with dark blue and lead gray. What was that old song? "Oh, it's cloudy in the west, and it's lookin' like rain, and my damned old slicker's in the wagon again." It did seem like most of the rain in this part of the country came from the west and southwest. They were saying that rainfall was already shy three or four inches this spring, and rain was as precious to grazing land as to farm land.

He mused about Izzy and Johnny. Down south in the old days, maybe still in Chihuahua and Sonora, maybe even now on the King Ranch in the tip of Texas, there was a *hacienda* system with a *patron* and a bunch of *peons.* The *patron* was respected because he was an aristocrat and at the same time his own best hand, and the good ones always had the interest of the *peons* in mind. Here on the Woodstock Ranch was a strange twist. The *patron* and lady *patron* here were *Latinos* and the *peons* were *Anglos.* Not much aristocracy, but there was no question as to who was the boss of the ranch and who was the main woman.

Izzy was like a mother to the ranch. She cooked and cleaned and canned food as if this were the center of a community. She kept many of the old ways but gloried in the luxury of the washing machines and the refrigerator and the freezers and electrical appliances and gas fuel. It was a wonder she did not adopt a bunch of people in the town of Woodstock to take care of.

The chickens, not long off their roosts, were gathered around their drinking pans at the windmill nearest the house. The pans were covered with slatted frames of wood so that livestock would not disturb them. Roosters diligently chased hens around and sometimes caught one and did their morning duty.

Old Gabe came out from under the house porch and approached George with tail wagging as if to say, "Whatever you mean to do, I'll help you."

The dog did help around the place. At one time he had decided that no wild bird, blackbird, mockingbird, sparrow, scissortail, quail, or whatever, should drink the chickens' water, but Papa had taught him that it was all right. Now the dog protected the place only from coyotes and other varmints. He was a good cow dog. The main responsibility he felt now was to make sure that the two milk cows reported out of the horse pasture to the milk pen gate in the evening. They were usually prompt, but, if not, Gabe was nipping and barking at their heels. The same way with their two calves, which ran free at night, learning to graze; they had to report to the milk pen gate when Johnny came out the back door with milk buckets in his hands.

The old dog stayed outside most of the time, but he knew the rules. If it was freezing cold, he could come inside to Papa's bedroom. And if the big fireplace was burning and Papa was alone in the library reading, he could come in and rest his head on the old man's feet. After Papa went to the nursing home, Gabe had taken the privilege of going sometimes to Homer's room, as if the halfwit boy was close kin to old Franklin Woodstock and would understand the agreement.

Looking at the conglomeration of buildings and lots and pens in the barn area, remembering the talk of the night before, George mused about his father. The old man was a builder, even built too much probably. Who would have guessed about those poems, if he did really write them? One thing for certain, Papa was practical. He remembered one time, pouring the concrete foundation for a chicken house, Papa had said that in a three-four-five triangle the point opposite the long side is always a right angle, so you can use the idea to make square corners. How much along that line did the old man know?

He, George, believed that he could have been a good ranch manager if he had stayed at home and worked at it. And Papa could have been a good metal worker. Also Johnny. It was a matter of being practical.

The outbuildings were of different construction and appearance. Most were the gray color of weathered wood; the tall barn with a loft was painted dull red; the long equipment shed was made of galvanized corrugated steel sheets. Those which had an open side opened on the south; they let a little spring rain blow in, but blocked the northers in winter. The pens and loading chute and stacklot fence were of cedar posts and lumber. Papa did not like to use pipe fences unless he had to, and he did not like to use mesquite posts around a barn.

In the stacklot were only two stacks, one of bundled sorghum, one of bundled oats, each about ten feet wide, twelve or fourteen high, and sixty long. They were carefully put together, with the grain inside and the butts out. A tarp on top protected the center from rain. Horses and milk cows would not eat the fodder this time of year when grass was good, but, if given a bundle, would carefully nibble off the grain.

The long equipment shed sheltered a mixture of old and new machinery: two pickups, only one of which would run. A horse trailer. Two tractors, one of which was fitted with attachments front and rear to pick up and dump dirt. An old wagon with wooden wheels and iron rims. A drill twelve feet wide for sowing wheat or oats. Plows, planters, cultivators. An ancient grain binder which had not worked in thirty years. A truck which, fitted with its sideboards, would haul a dozen or more yearlings. And equipment of which no one knew the use except Papa, and maybe Johnny.

The mixture of things under the metal shed was something like Papa's way of running the ranch, the old mixed with the new. Papa actually favored tried and proven ways, but he slowly tested new methods. One thing he was strongly against, helicopters, which some larger ranches were using to inspect and even drive cattle. Papa claimed that the blamed contraptions scared the cows and that if anybody couldn't ride a horse, he should get out of the cow business.

Johnny came down to the barn area, and George helped him load some yellow salt blocks into the pickup. One of Papa's theories was that if you had a draw or a hillside which was not being grazed enough, you should put out salt to lure the stock, and he always put out the yellow blocks so that a cow could see them from a half a mile away. Johnny was uncertain about putting out the salt now because of the possibility of rain, but he needed to shut down a couple of windmills anyway. He had already called Slim and Buck to shut down the windmills to the south if the wind got gusty. He drove away north.

Most of the dozen or so earth tanks on the place had a drilled well nearby. A water sand lay only eighty or ninety feet below the surface. The windmills pumped into watering troughs of concrete, except for a couple, again mixing the new and the old, which were built of old whitened cypress planks. The troughs overflowed into a pipe or a ditch and ran into the earth tanks. With this system the stock always had drinking water even if it did not rain for months. The windmills ran continually unless the earthen tanks were full, and they took a lot of care, greasing and repairing.

Johnny had been able to spend so much time searching because, fortunately, the spring roundup was complete before the old man ran away from the nursing home. Papa had always said that the last freeze is March 20, and spring branding will start the first week in April. They could always hire a couple of old experienced stove-up cowhands in town and two or three stout youngsters who wanted to play cowboy. The pay was thirty dollars a day and grub. They branded, earmarked, and vaccinated the heifer calves in chutes but roped and threw the bull calves in the old way so that they could be cut.

They branded a "standing W" on the right hip and cut the left ear in a swallow fork. In the spring all the calves old enough to live on grass were separated from their mothers into another pasture. At the fall roundup in October, they would be sold at about six-hundred pounds. Johnny still had fifty head of steers he had carried since the previous fall on a field of winter wheat. He had said that they ought to go to eight-hundred pounds and bring sixty-five cents a pound on the hoof.

The ranch was cross-fenced into a number of separate pastures, and four different locations had lumber pens and loading chutes. For fifty years Papa had been selling range delivery. The buyers brought their trucks out and got help with the loading.

The hands on the Woodstock now rarely ever rode horseback very far, but carried their mounts in horse trailers to where they were needed. Then they came back to the big house for the mid-day meal. They were free to sleep in the old bunkhouse if they wanted, in which case they got breakfast and supper also.

Clarence came out the back door before noon. George said, "Hey! Don't you know we get up at five-thirty on this ranch?"

"Is that right? I thought that was about the time we went to bed. It must have been that cheap beer you fed me. When in the devil do you sleep?"

"Can't sleep in the daytime," George said. "You kept me up too late last night."

They ate lunch. The clouds in the west looked even darker and seemed to be nearer. A smell of rain was in the air. They thought it best, if they were going to the Woodstock Cemetery, to go ahead. It was only a twenty-minute drive, just north of town.

Riding out that way in the Pontiac, they were quiet until Clarence suddenly said, "We really shouldn't do this, you know."

"How's that?"

"Suppose we find a grave, and Papa arranged his own burial. We shouldn't dig it up. Even if he was getting childish, he had a right to make a decision."

"We'll just keep it between us," George said.

The graveyard, fenced with sheep wire, was grown up with grass and weeds. The gravestones looked bleak sticking up through the dry grass of the year before. Here and there a path led toward someone's final resting place. At their mother's grave, Clarence said, "You know, we have to get a few flowers. Is there still a place in town?"

They went back to town. At the nursery and flower shop they bought a red pot of something which might have been iris or lilies. Back at the cemetery they put it on the washed mound behind the marble stone. She had been gone thirty-five years, and George could hardly picture her in his mind anymore.

Dust rose out of the knee-high grass as they walked around. George thought, *Funny how you bury people and are certain they will stay green in your memory, but they do not.* With the stones sticking up in the light of the cloudy day, the place seemed neither peaceful nor disturbed, but only mysterious. The whitish markers were like standing ghosts, wrapped in their pasts, waiting for nothing.

Clarence flushed a clutch of baby quail. They watched the mother bird flopping and fluttering along the ground, making small cries, pretending to have a broken wing, while her babies scurried to find the darkest hiding place they could.

They found only two mounds which had been made in recent months. One was obviously for a baby. The other was already marked with a stone for Samuel Smythe, who was from one of the old settler families. They satisfied themselves that Papa could not have been secretly buried here, and they seemed equally ready to leave.

In town Clarence said, "Let's drive over to the county line and get some beer. Somebody drank all ours up last night."

George agreed. This was a dry county. It was a fifteen-minute drive to the county line, where a big red neon sign had proclaimed "Beer" as long as they could remember. They bought a case, which Clarence insisted on paying for.

By the time they got out to the ranch the wind was gusty, and big drops of rain were blowing in the air. They saw Johnny down at the equipment shed and walked down to see if they could help do anything. The three came under the shed just in time to escape a flurry of rain. Old Gabe came bounding in to join them.

Johnny motioned west where the clouds were a mixture of dead gray and green. "Hail. I just put Old Baldy and Old Hickory in a stall. They don't have enough sense to come in out of the weather."

Thunder rumbled and lightning crackled, but little rain fell. Johnny said, "Just our luck if it all goes north of us and south of us. That's happened twice already this spring. What we need is a slow drizzling rain."

The wind ebbed and surged. A couple of mesquites and a stiff old oak swayed and jerked back and forth. Johnny said, "I hope to hell Slim and Buck got those other windmills shut down. This will whip them to pieces." The two windmills toward the house were stopped, their fan blades turned endways to the wind, but they swayed back and forth.

Hail hit with a sudden clatter on the metal building. The white balls were not large, as big as a marble or the end of a man's thumb. They bounded and rolled on the ground wildly. Their sound grew to a roar on the roof. There was no point in the three men trying to talk; it was impossible. They grinned and frowned, realizing that they had picked the worst place anywhere around for a refuge.

Two gray barn cats sneaked into the shed about a hundred feet away. They watched the hail and Gabe. The old dog stared at them as if to say, just keep your place, you varmints. The cats were part of a family which had stayed around the outbuildings more than half a century, keeping the mice and rats in check.

The beating on the metal roof was savage. It seemed to insist that everybody pay attention. For some reason, George pictured the cemetery where they had been earlier. He saw the standing stones and the overgrown grass beaten in the hailstorm. Those buried there, they knew this life in this country and had seen and heard these early summer storms.

He thought of a time in '44 when they had flown down to Palmyra near Christmas Island. There was an intertropical front close to the equator. The pilot veered right or left, trying to miss the most angry-looking cumulonimbus clouds. The lumbering old Liberator bomber bucked and swayed, dipped and yawed, and the crew felt the one g of gravity go back and forth from zero to two. Hail sounds on the fusilage covered up the constant roar of the engines. Navigation, following the pilot's erratic course, was difficult, but George knew that it was all-important. He worked as quick and cool as he could until they would come through to blue sky and calm water.

Around the top gun turret in the ceiling of the flight deck water leaked in and fell on his chart, but he paid no attention. A large part of the impression at that time seemed to come from the vast stretches of unknown wilderness ocean. But now, well over forty years later, it seemed clear that the big feeling, half fear and half wonder, came from large forces in the air and the earth, whether on land or sea.

Funny how you think strange thoughts at a time like that. The storm was over as suddenly as it began. The melting hailstones lay in thin drifts along the ground. Johnny estimated that it amounted to less than a half inch of rain.

Back in the big house George called collect back to Helen and to Fowler at the shop. He would not be able to get home today, but would make it tomorrow for sure.

Frank had spent the day exploring his grandfather's library, and at supper he talked with enthusiasm about the thousands of books; there was even a lot of basic geology. Homer poked food into his mouth and watched the others. Clara and Annie had gone back to town.

Johnny looked at the two, George and Clarence, almost with apology, and asked, "Could we have a talk? It's about a plan Papa had, and I don't think Walter understands."

They sat in the library. Clarence brought in some beer. Johnny agreed to drink one. Frank wandered along the shelves, mumbling the titles.

"What it is," Johnny said, "Walter called a couple of times, and he talks about doing something with the ranch. He says even if we find Papa he won't be in shape to decide things. I think Walter is a smart guy and all, but he doesn't understand this project Papa had for eighty years.

"We've got two hundred head of heifers out there in the northeast pasture. Two years old. Ready to be bred. I wouldn't say what they're worth to us, but it's a hell of a lot more than they're worth for beef or to anybody else. They are the bloodline for this exact ranch.

"No breeding cows have been brought on this place since Papa was a little boy. They were the original Longhorn stock that ran wild down south of here for two or three hundred years. But blooded Hereford bulls have been put on the females all along. You switch pastures with the bulls or trade them or sell them for bologna, so they don't breed their own offspring and you get too much inbreeding.

"You cull the mother cows in the fall, the ones that are not in good shape to go through the winter. And if a cow has come up with a calf with red spots on his face or a ring around one eye, you ship her out. Or if she had a miscarriage. Also, you try to remember if she has a daughter in the breeding herd; you cull the daughter. Papa could remember which cow was another cow's calf.

"But the cows that produce and raise good calves, you save their heifer calves. You slowly improve the herd. They are nearly fullblood Herefords now, but they have a little strain of Longhorn you can't see. They fit this land.

"Papa stayed away from the Angus and Brahmas and these new breeds on purpose, so our stock won't win any ribbons at the stock show, but they bring top prices on the market. And they fit the land. The exact grass and plants on this place, they know them from generations back. The weather suits them, dry times and gully-washer rains, northers and 105 degrees in the shade."

As if he was a little embarrassed at making such a long talk, Johnny said in a lighter tone: "You know what I think those two hundred heifers did when it came that hail? They just humped their back and went on grazing. Maybe one of them says, 'What we really need is a good, long drizzling rain.'"

They laughed. Clarence said, "Then another one says, 'When are they going to turn in the bulls?'"

In a minute Johnny said, "You can see what I'm trying to say. We couldn't buy those heifers any place, and we couldn't buy their mother cows out there in the herd. Nobody else would pay what they're worth to this ranch. If you lose them, it would take fifty to a hundred years to get them back again."

George said, "It seems plain that the heifers should be kept. What does that mean in regard to changing the operation around here?"

"Not a thing. Just keep on doing what Papa did. You look at the pastures in the fall and figure how many head they will carry through the winter. Then you cull down to that number."

At the same time that he understood and sympathized with Johnny's ideas, George was wondering how he might take out the capital for his shop. He could not guess what Clarence was thinking. The three of them generally agreed, though the specter of Walter with his management ability and ego loomed large. To say nothing of Irma.

Johnny and Frank went to bed. George said, "You're not going to keep me up all night tonight, little brother. One more beer, then I hit the sack."

Clarence agreed: one more, two at most. They began to ask about each other's kids. Clarence said that Dorothy and her husband were in Alaska; he had not seen them in three years. They were thinking about taking up a homestead when he got out of the Air Force. Margaret's husband was still in prison; the parole board had passed him by again. Of course, he got to see Frank and his kids a lot.

George reported that Melvin was still in Tulsa. Jimmy Lee was working for some shipping company in Houston and, nearly forty years old, was planning to go back to school to get his law degree.

They agreed not to brag too much on their grandkids. George said he never got to see his.

"That's one thing that's wrong with this country today," Clarence said. "Kids don't get to see their grandparents. Talk about mobility. People are scattered every which way. In this hectic modern world the friendship of an older person, either grandparent or great-grandparent, would be of importance to the psychological health of the child. Primitive people used to understand this better than we do."

Clarence paused, chuckled a little, and said, "You know, changing the subject—both Walter and Irma insist that they are like Papa, or even that Papa is like them. I guess that peculiar Dobbs started that train of thought. Well, thinking about all these books, maybe I'm the most like Papa. I've got nearly half that many books myself."

"I thought Papa got the books for Homer, to keep him from breaking into the school library. Even if he can't understand a word he reads."

"I wouldn't be sure he doesn't understand."

"Well, as for being most like Papa, Clara is the only one that's had sense enough to stay around here instead of moving into the hustle and bustle around a big city."

"*Touché,* George. But back to Homer—he may be an idiot-savant. He has his wires crossed in his head so that his balance is bad and things sometimes seem to be upside down. Also it's a motor function disorder. But they have found people who made an impression like Homer does, and yet are especially competent in some things. They surprise people. The boy is lucky to have someone like Papa, who seems to understand, and Clara, who is a very competent grandmother, and Izzy, who is a damned good cook."

"I agree," George said. "Say, do you remember when Clara was about twelve or so and she tried to give herself a permanent with some of those old curling irons that look like a pair of scissors? You stick them down in the globe of a lamp to get hot, then roll up pieces of hair on the hot part."

"Yeah. She really messed up her hair."

"Burnt about half of it off, in spots here and there.

Mother fixed her a shawl to tie over her head so she could go to school."

"Yeah. Remember those dust storms?"

"And those prickly pear and catclaws and devil's pincushions?"

"And those centipedes and stinging scorpions?"

"Yeah. Say, I'm sitting here about asleep. What say we hit the hay?"

Next morning Frank brought the *Banner* back from town. It had been published a couple of days before. In it was a long article about Franklin Woodstock and his mysterious disappearance from the local nursing home.

The editor had grown flowery in his writing. The search for this great western pioneer had grown worldwide. Detectives were searching the nooks and crannies in every direction for Franklin Woodstock, the well-known local rancher.

Papa's civic conscience was lauded. He had always contributed generously to the Boy Scouts, the Salvation Army, the United Business Men's Club, and the Baptist Church. He had once contributed to the cost of new football helmets for the Woodstock High School team. He had been a fighting hero in World War I. The editor had it wrong about the age; Papa was ninety one, instead of ninety eight.

The article noted that the immediate family was not available for interview because of their searching and their concern, but officials at the Goodhaven Nursing Home had been fully cooperative. The administrator and the director of nursing had reported that Franklin Woodstock had been a model patient, and all the nurses and aides loved to care for him. They supposed that he had departed the Goodhaven institution because he did not wish to be any trouble to anybody.

The article mentioned Walter, a highly successful New York businessman, and Clara, a local lady, and Ed Bender, a grandson and proprietor of the local hardware store.

About noon Ed Bender called. Clarence talked to him. The man seemed to have some kind of emergency and said he sure needed to see George and Clarence. They drove into town and parked in front of the hardware store.

They had no sooner closed the doors of the old Pontiac than they noticed the mess on the plate glass at the store front. Crude, hasty letters in white paint proclaimed: Old Woodstock Is a Skunk. He Got My Grandpa's Land for Peanuts.

Ed was in the store alone and had his usual worried look. Clarence asked, "Is that all they did? What else did they do?"

"Oh, that's all. No problem."

"Can you clean the glass?"

"Oh, sure, Uncle Clarence. It's just whitewash. They got it down at the newspaper office too last night, and they already got it cleaned up."

George said, "I thought you had some kind of trouble."

"I'm in bad trouble." He motioned them back toward the large room at the rear.

Two tables were littered with papers—scraps of notebook paper with scribbled figures, a dozen pamphlets spread open, forms partially filled out, ledgers, receipts, bills, cancelled checks.

"I'm in trouble," he repeated. "Where I got hung up and nearly blew my top is worrying about what is recovery property and non-recovery property. They keep changing the rules and the forms. I've got an extension from IRS, but what good does that do me? A damned bookkeeper who is supposed to do taxes looked at my records and he estimated it would cost a thousand dollars. A thousand dollars!

"Uncle Clarence, you're an expert in English. You could read the instructions and explain it to me and tell me what it is they're trying to say. I can't make heads and tails out of it. Seems like I can read anything but what these government guys write.

"And, Uncle George, you're good at math. You always were good at math. You're a surveyor and a navigator. You can figure a fifteen percent declining balance and not bat an eye. I've added up a bunch of numbers a dozen times and got a different answer every time. You all could help me and fix the whole mess in a day or two."

George and Clarence were equally surprised and dubious and reluctant.

George asked, "Have you cheated on your income taxes?"

"I don't know. I didn't pay the September estimated tax. Once last year I took a drill motor out of stock and used it at home a couple of days, but I sold it for a new tool. And I charged off the pickup for business, and I took it fishing with some guys last spring. They trade here, but this is the only hardware store in town, and I didn't have to take them fishing. Then I might have used some stamps bought for business to mail a personal letter."

Clarence tried to reassure him. "All you need to do is fill it out the best you can. The IRS will accept your best honest effort."

"No, Uncle Clarence, that bookkeeper that wanted a thousand dollars, he nearly went all the way through law school, and he said you could get in the federal pen at Leavenworth for income taxes. I know the feds are already looking at me because I applied for this extension away back by the middle of April. I need help. All my figures showed I made more than ten thousand in this store last year for salary and profit, and I don't know where it went. It just don't add up."

The man was serious. Although the matter seemed ridiculous, the amount of papers spread out on the two tables and the look on his face indicated that he was serious.

George said, "You've got a calculator over there. You sure don't need anybody to do the arithmetic for you."

"Well, what about this, Uncle George? I added it all up and had seventy pounds of ten penny nails to start with, then I sold fourteen pounds, then the inventory at the end of the year shows twenty pounds. How do you put that down? People come in here and pay cash, and I don't make out a receipt. I just find out I've got more money than the books say. I had one check for forty dollars bounce for insufficient funds and never did get paid. How do you add that up? Old lady Winks bought a roto-tiller and I got it from the factory and she wouldn't pay the freight and that's not all; she got the blades so bound up with roots it wouldn't run, and the factory wouldn't fix it, and I had to pay a mechanic twenty-eight dollars to take it all apart."

After a moment of silence Clarence asked, "What's that got to do with income tax?"

"Well, how do you put down the twenty-eight dollars? Is it depreciation or deduction or what? You and Uncle George can straighten these things out."

George tried to sound as final as he could. "I don't know about Clarence, but I went through all this torture in February, and I don't intend to do it again this summer. I wouldn't touch your tax forms with a ten-foot pole." He was sorry as soon as he said it.

Clarence tried to reassure the man. The Internal Revenue Service was not sending people to prison as long as they did their best. He, himself, did not understand the instructions, though he had a doctorate in English literature. George relented, and the two of them explained at length that he had to fill out the forms with his best guesses, send in any money he seemed to owe, and write the IRS a letter telling them all his problems, everything he had been talking about. Half the people at IRS did not understand the forms themselves and were guessing most of the time. The letter would undoubtedly prevent any further action by the government.

They escaped from Ed Bender as soon as they could.

"Takes after his mother," Clarence said.

George said, "Well, I don't know. Clara may be a dingbat, but she never was a whiner."

They picked up Frank, and George was glad to head the Pontiac east toward home. He had overstayed his intended visit and knew he was behind at the shop.

CHAPTER THIRTEEN

The Earth Mother

FOR a week George was buried in his shop work, hoping and expecting that he would not need to go back west again till the middle of August. He thought a lot about how Clarence and he had got along, how good it had been to talk to him. They had avoided going into the details of Clarence's son-in-law in prison and into the details of George's son Melvin's divorce and stiff child support payments. They had not talked about Clarence's son and a couple of his nephews by marriage who had died in Vietnam in what had come to seem a useless war. Clarence was just a friendly, easygoing guy. The man contradicted George's long conviction that people who are not practical—over-educated people, intellectuals, are worthless.

A job came in for bid in the shop, and he noted immediately that the dimensions were in centimeters. Fowler suggested they could just convert to inches and thousandths and go ahead and do the job. But George said, "See the machine screws that are called out? You got any metric taps and dies?"

"Nope."

"Well, that engine lathe out there won't cut metric threads either. We'll let some other sucker bid in the job."

"Maybe metric is the wave of the future."

"It might be. Maybe a couple of years down the road, when we get going good, we'll tool up for it."

That afternoon at home, trying to get his contrary lawn mower to start, he thought about how it is that things seem to get more hectic all the time: conveniences like this lawn mower that wear you out getting them to run, great so-called advances like the metric system. Keys. He had keys to the garage, back door, front door, the lock on the backyard gate, the Pontiac, the shop, shop pickup, tool boxes, luggage, and several that might or might not fit anywhere or somewhere. Credit cards. Companies sent credit cards all the time. He carefully cut his up. Helen proudly kept hers; she used the Gulf and the Sears and the Penny's. Neiman-Marcus did not send her one, thank God! Junk mail. Junk phone calls. Offers to let you win a million dollars. Made you wonder what the world is coming to.

The mower simply would not start. Helen thought the neighbors had begun to frown at the lawn, but they would just have to frown. Maybe Sunday afternoon he would tear it down, sand the rust off the magneto magnets, put in a new spark plug, adjust the carburetor.

Walter called at eight o'clock in the evening. Surprisingly he did not want to be picked up and hauled to Woodstock but was already there. "I'm at the Hi-Way Motel at the north edge of town," he said. "I flew in and rented an automobile. I needed to go over some of the findings of the accountant. I was wondering if you could drive over early in the morning. It would be just as well if you didn't go out to the ranch."

"What's the problem, Walter?"

"There are two problems. The bills from the Goodhaven Nursing Home seem excessive. But more important, my accountant has found from ranch and bank records a serious discrepancy. Some money is missing. I want an explanation. That's why I'm not staying at the ranch. I don't want to be dependent on Izzy and Johnny."

"What do you need me for?"

"I've asked Johnny to come in at ten o'clock in the morning. I'd like to have another family member present. I want you to understand any action we may find it necessary to take. Clara will not do. You know how she dotes on Johnny and Izzy."

"What time?"

"Ten o'clock."

"Okay. I'll see if I can get loose."

He had agreed to go, not merely because he wanted to know the problem but because it was plain that he estimated Johnny different from the way the eldest brother did.

Driving west in the early morning, the determination stayed in his mind that there should be no argument if he could stop it. Also he thought about problems in the shop and cursed the highway signs and the big trucks that hogged the road. He made the drive in a little under three hours and pulled up to the Hi-Way Motel at a few minutes till ten. It was one of those fancy places for traveling salesmen and tourists, with a restaurant and swimming pool.

Walter had a suite at the motel, with waxed woodwork and stuffed leather couch and chairs. George asked at once, "Where's Johnny?"

"He'll be here in fifteen minutes."

"What's the matter? A ten dollar discrepancy in the accounts?"

"It's no joking matter. My accountant has gone back three years in cancelled checks and income tax returns. Deposits, purchases, everything. There is forty thousand dollars spent for nothing that makes sense. Forty thousand!" Walter sounded belligerent.

George was thinking that his brother always seemed to need to put on an imposing front and must surely be a tyrant to people working for him. He remembered hearing someone say that the most cutthroat businessmen in New York were those transplanted from places like Texas.

George asked, "How do you know about the forty thousand?"

"A cancelled check. Made out to some outfit in New Mexico which I never heard of. It's not listed as business expense or charity."

"Signed by Johnny?"

"Made out and signed by Johnny and countersigned by Papa."

"Papa? Then what's the problem? Do you object to Papa spending his own money?"

"Don't fight me, George. Anybody knows that an old man over eighty can be taken advantage of."

"How long ago was this check dated?"

"A little over two years."

"Well, Walter, only a few months ago Papa had this catscan, whatever it is, and you know about it. Isn't that legal evidence that he knew what he was doing?"

"Don't fight me, George. Listen, sit down. I'm a professional manager and happen to be making some sacrifice of time and energy for the benefit of the five heirs of Papa's estate. I'm not out to embarrass Johnny. If this money is salary owed to him and Izzy, then okay. But two things: One, we know it's paid, and two, we know the estate paid taxes on a business expense which it should not have paid. George, I need your backing to handle this, and all I want from Johnny is a true and complete explanation."

"I'm not going to back you if you're going to jump on him. You know we have to have him to run the ranch."

"Dammit, George, we must have him right now, but only until we dispose of this substantial property. Do you object to his accounting for forty thousand dollars?"

"No, if you don't make him mad."

They sat there in silence until Johnny came in. George

was thinking how much more at ease he felt with the young Chicano than with his own stern and polished older brother.

When Johnny came in, Walter went to what was evidently a bar cart furnished by the motel. "What would you gentlemen like to drink? Scotch?"

Johnny said, "No, thanks."

George asked, "You haven't got a cold beer in there?"

Walter held up two bottles of expensive imported beer, and Johnny agreed to have one too. Walter poured them into glasses and mixed himself a drink of hard liquor, then paced back and forth as he spoke.

"Johnny, we have run into a problem, a puzzle. You understand that we have to check up on all these accountants and bookkeepers. About two years ago a check was made out for forty thousand, without any explanation. I'm sure that you can understand that the accountants need exact, explicit facts."

Johnny did not bat an eye for half a minute. Then he said slowly, "It's a long story, Walter."

"That's what we need, the complete story. That's all we want, complete details." Walter sat down and laced his fingers together on the front of his vest.

"Well, I'll try to tell it. There is this small Indian tribe in New Mexico. That's their home now, but it was in Arizona before that. They always listened to the wise old men. The old men ran the tribe. Sometimes they wandered around and sometimes they stayed a hundred years at a good farm spot by a river; then they might follow after piñon nuts or deer or antelope or east to the buffalo. But when they came to a dangerous time for the tribe, if the old wise men couldn't agree, they had to find the queen. It was hard to find her, because they had to ask questions of everybody about their ancestors. They might go two hundred years without needing to find the queen. Then. . . ."

"Excuse me," Walter said. "Wait a minute. I'm sure there is a point to this." He took a calm drink of his scotch and set the bare glass back down on the varnished end table. George thought how Helen would give him hell for making rings like that on a wooden table.

Walter pronounced, "Indians do not have queens."

Johnny was not intimidated but was sincerely trying to explain. "The word cannot be translated. I can't even pronounce it. Some of the tribe now calls her the queen. The word means a special woman you find and ask what to do when the people are in trouble. I think the long Indian word also tells you how you know which woman. The Anglos don't have such a woman, so they don't have a word for her. She is kind of like the Earth Mother, if the Earth Mother were a person.

"She must be the descendant of a queen who answered at least a hundred years ago. She must have kin in all the four clans of the tribe. She must have lived or visited at least two winters with foreign people, more if possible. There are other things they have to ask about her ancestors.

"They don't find the queen unless the old men can't decide what to do. Like one time long ago they lost the corn seed, and some wanted to just roam, and some wanted to attack other people and steal the seed. They found the queen, and she told them to trade dried squash and dried pumpkin for new corn seed. Another time they found the queen, and she told them they must teach the children to speak Spanish."

George was thinking that Walter was getting a lot more "complete story" than he really wanted. It was strange that Johnny, one worn boot cocked up on the other knee, trying to explain sincerely, had the upper hand over the well-educated brother.

"We were in the big room," he said. "Papa and I were just inside the door, standing there watching. They were squatting down on their heels around her, about a dozen old men, around her sitting in that rocking chair. The electric lights were not turned on, just a coal oil lamp on the long mantel. You know how Mother always burned that coal oil lamp nearly all night. Papa and I heard . . . ."

Walter was aggravated. "Wait a minute! What the hell are you talking about? What happened to the Indians? I'm trying to be patient with your long story. What happened?"

"They found the queen."

"Are you trying to say Izzy?"

"Yes, my mother."

Walter asserted, "Izzy is a Mexican."

Johnny did not object to his mother being called Izzy; he was used to it. He did not assert but had a certain integrity in his manner as he said, "What is a Mexican!"

It was not a question, and Walter was at a loss. He seemed just on the verge of saying something without knowing what it would be.

Johnny said, "A Spaniard came up through Northern New Spain, through New Mexico and Texas and Oklahoma, and was camping in Kansas seventy years before the Pilgrim fathers in the Mayflower landed at Plymouth Rock. History has not explained certain things very well."

George was surprised at the knowledge and assurance of the Chicano cowhand as Johnny went on. "The last queen was a cousin to the first vice-president of Texas."

Walter's board-room demeanor did not seem to be adequate. He appeared uncertain and unwilling, yet resigned to hearing the strange story.

"It was funny," Johnny said. "But not the kind of funny to laugh at. That dim lamp and her sitting there and them all squatting around her. Papa and I stood back, not even whispering to each other. I couldn't hardly believe it.

"Long ago they had a kind of underground room called a kiva. It's not their word, but they borrowed it from another people. It's a holy place. No woman could come in the kiva except the queen maybe every hundred years. I thought this was like that holy place. There Mother sat in her chair, rocking a little bit, slowly; it made a tiny creaking noise. In the dim light you could see those thousands of books lined up around the walls.

"Their children went to a school of the Indian Bureau. Their problem was about the question if some must go away to universities. She told them that the ten best students must go away to universities and study law or agriculture or medicine or some kind of journalism. They must all promise to come back to the tribe later.

"But the old men's argument was about money. The students would work, but there had to be money for bus tickets and tuition and all that stuff. They could sell all the sheep and horses and the silver things for forty thousand dollars. Must they sell the sheep and horses and silver things?

"Mother rocked slowly. The old men waited and waited. Finally she looked at Papa. He shook his head no.

"That's all the story. She fed them steak and canned corn and canned peaches, and Papa told me to make out the check."

Walter by this time undoubtedly had drunk more scotch than he had intended, but he held it well. He said, "Well, now that Papa's gone, there must be no more such transactions without consulting me."

Johnny neither agreed nor disagreed. He had some fence to fix and would not stay.

After the younger man was gone, Walter paced some more. He mused, "It was a fool sucker thing to do. How long has Izzy been on the ranch?"

"I don't know," George said. "More than thirty years, I guess."

"Well, that just might be her salary. A hundred dollars a month plus board and room would be a good salary for a cook. Be sure and don't say anything to Johnny about its being counted salary. We don't want him to get any exaggerated ideas about salaries. Ye gods! no telling what a ranch manager gets these days. Above all, George, don't say anything about Izzy and Johnny getting a lawyer when we settle this business. A lawyer might open up the damndest can of worms, suspicion of a common-law marriage or no telling what."

Walter wanted him to go to the nursing home in the event that he needed some help to straighten out the atrocious bills charged against Papa. They went to the restaurant for lunch. Walter had a shrimp salad. George had a hamburger and another beer.

At the Goodhaven Nursing Home, George realized that he did not want to be a part of any more confrontations. He said, "I'll wait in the recreation room" and went on without waiting for a reply.

He found the place as he remembered it, a long room with big windows along the side looking out on the grass and oak trees. The few patients seated at the windows were watching a young man in blue jeans and no shirt moving the lawn. Two old women were playing dominoes. Several old people were dozing in their chairs.

George knew that it would be a while before Walter got straight with the office. As he walked toward an empty chair, a man sprang up smiling. It was the oral history man, Hap Albright.

"George Woodstock! Good to see you!"

George could not help smiling as he said hello.

Hap said, "They tell me you haven't located your father yet. Trying to get some more clues around here?"

George explained that he was waiting for his brother,

who was trying to straighten out some confusion about some bills.

They chatted a few minutes, and Hap waxed enthusiastic about his work. "You know, George, this oral history is fascinating, and I keep learning more and more about how to do it. If I live to be a hundred, maybe I'll learn all the subtle angles."

They laughed.

"It's not textbook history at all. You may have to guess at the time and place and the situation. You're looking for the human feeling, attitudes toward life. You know, George, I had a colleague who taught creative writing and he set out to write a realistic family saga. Said it was going to be a well-made novel. Further he went, the more he got frustrated. In-laws kept on intruding on his characters. He couldn't keep his ancestors and times and dates and occupations straight with public affairs and changing technology, much less keep his attitudes and temperaments straight. He said that families are without doubt the worst-made novels that exist. I guess he filed the manuscript in the round file on the floor by his desk."

"I know what he meant," George said. "I can't remember the names of all my wife's aunts and nephews, or even some of my own brother's and sister's kids."

"Well, oral history is simpler. Nothing well-made about it. You don't worry much about facts and don't even ask the subject to describe his feelings in the past. They'll tell you. You just fish around for interesting details. Old horse people—get them to remembering horses' names and how they got the names. Same with dogs they had. Do they remember the first automobile they ever saw; what did people say about it? Did their folks talk politics; what did they say about Teddy Roosevelt? Did anyone tell them ghost stories? What was the first job they ever had for pay?

"You know, George, you get the bright spots and dark spots of a life. You get ironies. Somehow it's important.

It's very difficult to visualize our parents and grandparents as children and young people, but they live with their childhood and youth deep inside them. Sometimes I get overly enthused about it, but Franklin Woodstock would be a great subject."

George said, "It would be up to Papa if we find him."

The older brother was angry when he came out of the office and did not have time to meet the oral history man. Out in the car he raved: Those idiots are like a bunch of Philadelphia lawyers. They will tell you everything but what you want to know. They say a patient threw a set of false teeth at a nurse and hit her in the eye. They caught a visitor smoking in a room where the patient was on oxygen. They say it takes two nurse's aides to get some patients up and give them a shower. They say some of the patients hear voices which no one else hears. None of it has anything to do with Papa's bills. I informed them in no uncertain terms that he is no longer a patient at the Goodhaven Nursing Home and they are not to reserve his room or make any more charges at all. They may get sued for allowing a patient to escape. I happen to have a couple of Connecticut lawyers just as devious as they are, and I just might get them down here to apply pressure where pressure is needed."

George declined to come into the motel and have a drink. There was just about time to get home before dark.

Driving east in the old Pontiac, he thought about the strange story about Izzy, the queen. It did seem funny, as Johnny had said, but not to laugh at. He believed it. She was something to those people, and maybe it didn't make sense, but it was true anyway. You can't tell what people are or where they've been or what they've done. As for Papa's suddenly giving away the forty thousand, that was easy to believe. The old man had told him he could have a hundred thousand when he was ready. Get the shop lined out and some employees you trust, a plan you're sure will work. Nothing about a loan or anything legal. Just say you're ready, and you can have the hundred thousand to finance some machine tools or whatever you need. As if to say, What is money for?

He was vaguely glad that the strange people had found the queen when Papa was still around to say yes.

CHAPTER FOURTEEN

Prairie Fire

He had worked hard all day in the shop of a competitor, using their hydraulic press to run off a bunch of parts for which he had built the tools. He had worked as fast as he could, because they charged him five dollars an hour for the use of the machine. Not having any equipment himself that any of the competition found worth renting, they seemed to think they could take advantage of him any time.

He had just sat down to a TV dinner of fish and corn fritters when a phone call came from Beaumont. The nasal voice was unmistakable; it was the detective Dobbs.

"Mr. George Woodstock, glad to get in touch with you. Private Investigator Dobbs here. You have not called in any information to my home office since I last spoke to you."

"I thought you were in Montana or some place."

"We follow up these leads until they play out; then we pick up the trail elsewhere. I believe your father was known to speak with nostalgia about the beautiful piney woods and the Big Thicket of East Texas. I've been searching these areas. Have you been able to remember any specific places in this wooded country that he wanted to visit in his old age?"

"Nope. Not especially."

"Your sister Irma has stated that he considered the tall trees like a temple. Did he speak of that to you?"

"Not to me, he didn't, Mr. Dobbs."

"Now, Mr. George Woodstock, your brother Clarence has mentioned that your father wrote poetry. I wonder why I wasn't informed about this before?"

"I don't know."

"Did he ever write a poem about beautiful country? I'm thinking about that semi-desert country where he ranched and wondering whether he looked back with regret toward a land which might be more favorable. Do you recall any poem he wrote about specific plants and trees in a less arid country?"

"Well, it doesn't seem like semi-desert to me out there, Mr. Dobbs. Here lately I've found out he might have written some poems, but I don't know whether it's true or not."

"Was his poetry about a more beautiful country? Did he write about trees and such?"

"Nope, he wrote about shooting craps."

"Well, now, Mr. George Woodstock, I understand that some vandalism occurred recently directed against your father. I have previously asked about the possibility of hatred or resentment around the West Texas town of Woodstock. I have tried to impress on you and others the absolute necessity of being frank and open with me, if I am to do my job. I wonder why I was not better advised about these matters?"

"Oh, hell, it was just some whitewash on my nephew's window and on the newspaper window. Some juveniles. You can't live around a town a long time without some people getting it in for you. It was not serious at all."

"There is no deep-seated hatred against your father?"

"No, there sure is not."

"Well, then, I have another question. Have you been able to locate any satisfactory photographs of Franklin Woodstock?"

"No, sir, I gave you the best ones I had."

"Out in the hot sun, did he favor wearing a white hat or a black hat?"

"I don't know. Nearly always outdoors he wore a sort of straw hat."

"Well, Mr. George Woodstock, I should inform you that I have recorded our conversation in case you wish to change anything or add anything."

"I figured you were."

"Please call my headquarters if you have anything to tell me."

"Okay, Mr. Dobbs."

The fellow seemed like an idiot or a comedian. His fish and corn fritters were cold.

The first week in July was hot. It came up over 100 degrees day after day. He had been busy, but finally found time to install the two evaporative coolers in the shop. It was just a matter of jerry-rigging some wiring and running copper tubing to each one from an outside faucet. The copper tubing had been patched several places with rubber tape but would last another season. The four guys in the shop cheered when he turned the coolers on.

That same day the bone man called from Boston. He said, "George, this is Oliver Overstreet. Do you have a few minutes to talk? Would it be better for me to call you at home this evening?"

George settled himself into his chair. "No, I have a few minutes."

"Fine. Fine. I remember that good visit with you. Don't forget that I owe you a case of beer."

"Okay."

"Just wanted to thank you, George, also wanted to keep in touch and make a little report on the project. We got our survey done and got pictures, also a dozen different kinds of fossils and later bones, which we found partially exposed. We even have some small fossilized bones which are tentatively identified as coming from the giant sloth and the saber-toothed tiger. Everything went along without a hitch, as they say. Now we are organizing the material to show the foundation people, the grant people." He chuckled as if it were a small joke.

George said, "One thing I probably forgot to mention when we talked. Down on the south end of that bluff is a point which looks like it would crack off any time. It's dangerous. We always stayed away from it."

"Right, George. We have certainly been aware of that point and have stayed away from it. Dr. Romer mentions that unstable section of Dead Cowbones Bluff in his notes made before 1930. Incidentally, a big piece of it has cracked off, evidently just from its own weight, this spring, not long before we were out there. But that area is not needed in our project, and we intend to stay away from it, down below and on top also."

"Well, I just wanted to make sure you know about it, Oliver."

"Fine. Fine. The whole project looks good. We have a small fly in the ointment, or some of these soft young professors think so. They have classes during the moderate weather, and it gets hot as blazes out there in the summer when they are off. Ha! They will just have to get a leave of absence or put up with the heat. Do you think it would be all right to begin our main dig next April?"

"I don't know. One thing, Johnny, the ranch manager, will do the spring roundup in April. I don't know if there would be any conflict."

"Fine. Fine. That's the kind of thing I need to know. We'll make sure there is no conflict and will project a starting date of the first of May. Our guarantee to the land owner will be the same as we made for the original survey. I gave you a copy of our policies, George. But we will add two provisions: One, we will fence off the area of our dig, although, as you have said, cattle do not graze there. It might be five acres, more or less. Two, we will fill in the trenches we dig and level the soil approximately as it is now. You understand that we may excavate as deep as ten feet in some places, but will fill it in. Do you have any other suggestions?"

"No, it sounds fair to me."

"Well, we just wanted to keep in touch. We are enthused and certainly appreciate your cooperation. One more thing, George. I . . . don't know that I should even mention it. It's not a complaint, but. . . ."

"What is it?"

"That boy, or young man. I guess they call him Homer. He has come around several times, but wouldn't let anyone come near him. If we waved or walked toward him, he would run and hide in some brush. If he wants to watch us, that's fine; we could give him a ride out to the dig. Just thought I'd mention it."

"It's all right, Oliver. He's harmless. Don't worry about it."

They hung up.

George lay awake that night mulling over the conversation and wondering. Dead Cowbones Bluff had been the same as long as he could remember, well over half a century. There had always been the dangerous point at the southern end, on the verge of caving. He and the other kids had thrown rocks from a distance, trying to make it give way. A few prods from below surely would have made it break off. And now it had finally done it, evidently not long after Papa disappeared from the nursing home.

His suspicions were crazy. Clarence had talked about an old Indian who had thrown himself away. But that was a fiction story. On the other hand, what about the poems? You could not figure out the poems from a practical old rancher. He remembered someone saying Papa could not be on the ranch, because Johnny had searched, and he knew the ranch better than any other person. And he had thought for one second that one person knew it better than Johnny.

George decided that he would try to put away the suspicion and not talk about it to any of the others.

During that hot July he got a lot of phone calls at home, from customers who wanted some advice, from one guy who wanted him to do some free machine work for a good cause, from hucksters selling burial insurance and financial advice. Near the end of the month Irma called from Atlanta just as he was settling into a comfortable chair after supper.

She was eager and insistent as usual. "George, it's so good to hear your voice. I have to ask you a big favor and I know I can depend on you."

He was thinking he would refuse to pick her up at the airport, but asked, "How is everything going?"

"It's Larry, George. He's the burden of my life, but he's trying to reform, and he told me you gave him some money, and I know you would want to do everything you can to help him reform. He got into a big fist fight with Wilbur, and they both had to go to the doctor. I don't blame Wilbur; he's so moral and has all the seminary training. But Larry is really trying to reform, and he will do it if we all pray for him and help him. I had to send him and his fiancee out to live with Clara."

"You what?"

"To live with Clara, George. I paid his fiancee Bonnie money for a bus ticket too if they would agree not to do anything intimate until after they're married. They think so much of each other. She's working part time to help them get by.

"Oh, George! I can't hardly bear to say it! Larry is living under a bridge out there at Woodstock. Bonnie is staying in a motel, and I'm sure it's because they don't want to do anything intimate before they're married, but Larry is living under a bridge!"

"Irma, I don't know whose idea it was to send him to Clara in the first place. She's a widow and getting old and I imagine she has all the problems she needs."

"Why, George, she has a veteran's pension from her husband and two rent houses that probably bring in three hundred a month. I trust Clara to take care of Larry, but that Ed Bender has stirred up all kinds of trouble. He has actually threatened Larry and has got the sheriff to threaten Larry. They have even gone so far as to threaten his fiancee also. That Ed Bender is just like Walter, with no feelings for his own blood kin. I know what's going on out there, because Larry calls me collect every two or three days. George, you can go out there and straighten things out. I cannot bear to think of Larry living under a bridge."

"Wait just a minute, Irma. What in the name of God was the idea of sending him out to Clara? Did she agree?"

"No, but I'm sure it would be a blessing to her. He is trying to reform, and we hope he will turn to the ministry in two or three years. Around a small town he will not be influenced by bad companions. Clara could keep him and his fiancee too; then Bonnie wouldn't have to work part time."

"What kind of work does Bonnie do?"

"She doesn't make much money. I imagine she sacks groceries or works at McDonald's or does housework. The money I gave them for bus tickets, they had to save it for food and they hitchhiked all the way to Woodstock. Can you imagine that? George, if they are not accepted at Clara's, I'll have to send them money to go out to Clarence in California. And maybe they don't have that good small-town feeling in California. I'm afraid they may fall in with bad companions in California."

He was wondering whether it was possible to find worse

companions than her son and his whore fiancee, but he said, "I don't understand the point in sending them to Clara. I've seen her lately, and it's plain that she doesn't need any more people to take care of and worry about. Why Clara?"

"Well, George, it's only two or three weeks till we all have to go out there and settle the estate. It seems like everyone has a scheme to use the ranch land, and I don't know if the worthwhile plans Wilbur and I have will prevail. We may not get the entire lands for the Christian retreat and the Noah's Ark plan. But think of this: there are five children. There is no way that Walter or anyone can prevent me from getting a fifth of the land. I have faith that these worthwhile projects will go forward. I have hopes that the heirs and the town will get behind our plans, and certainly there will be a place for Larry. I have told him to go to church and meeting and testify every chance he gets. There will be a place for Larry."

"Well, Irma, I'm against him living with Clara. I'm against it."

She said, "Then I don't know what to do. His father has a cousin that runs a bicycle repair shop in Toledo. I could send him and his fiancee there. Do you think Toledo would be better to reform him than California?"

"Sure. That's it, Sis. Send him to Toledo."

Somehow the issue had worked itself out. He did not want to insult his younger sister, but only wanted her to get off his back, and off his older sister's back.

Three days later Johnny called from the ranch at about nine in the morning. The ranch manager sounded tired. "George, we've got a problem out here, a grass fire. I thought you would want to know about it."

"Is it still burning? How far is it from the ranch house?"

"It's not close to the ranch house. It's mostly over on the Pendleton east of here. Me and Slim and Buck stayed up all night saving some of our fence."

"Can you get any help in town, Johnny?"

"We hired a couple of helpers. The fire truck and a lot of men that could get loose in town have gone out on the Pendleton. They've lost a lot of grass over there. They've started killing yearlings and skinning them half out, tying on with two ropes from saddle horns and dragging it along the fire front. You know how tight the Pendletons are, so they must think it's serious to make them waste beef."

"How are you fighting it?"

"Wet tow sacks. Carry a couple of barrels of water in a pickup."

"Look, Johnny, do you need me?"

"It's hard to tell. Maybe not if the wind doesn't change. I tell you what I need: somebody to take care of Clara and Homer and Annie. They won't leave the ranch and they're worried, and Mother is busy cooking; she has been feeding some of the men from the Pendleton even."

"Okay, Johnny, I'll be out there this afternoon."

He called Helen at home, had a short conference with Bob Fowler, and headed west.

It was one of those late July days, no clouds, a little dry wind from the south. The sky was like newly cut brass. He was lucky to have the sun overhead instead of in front. Even so, the highway made a person's eyes water if he kept on looking at it without blinking. Probably some people up north thought air conditioning in a car is a luxury. The air conditioning in the old Pontiac was a luxury this time of year about like three meals a day is a luxury.

They were not calling it a drouth, but it had not rained much in West Texas. Probably the early grass was now dry as tinder. He remembered a couple of small prairie fires and especially how Papa had been concerned and cautious about fire. Probably some town dudes had slipped into the

Pendleton Ranch to hunt quail or to fish in a stock tank and had thrown a burning cigar butt into the grass.

Going through the town of Woodstock he could see a bank of yellow and gray smoke out to the southwest. Out on the ranch road he estimated that still not much fire had come onto Woodstock land. A scattering of sunflowers brightened the prairie, now brown under August heat.

Johnny, Slim, and Buck, with two other workers, were filling water barrels in the back of two pickups at the windmill nearest the house. Clara, Homer, and Annie were standing watching. The men, who evidently had only got a few hours sleep, had dirty clothes and red eyes.

Johnny, sending Slim off with one of the men, told the two, "Go out where Plum Creek crosses into the Woodstock. Watch for fire close to the fence. You can go over there and help them if it looks like it's going to burn down to the creek bottoms. If it gets in that timber we sure can't do anything with wet tow sacks. We'll go back out where we were last night. And, Slim, they're coming over to our tank out there to fill up the fire truck. Watch them and make sure those town boys shut the gate."

George did not ask whether he was needed at the fire front; there had been a sort of agreement between them when Johnny called him. After the men were gone, Clara said, "I'm so glad you came. I promised Izzy to go to the grocery store for her, but it looked hopeless to take these two rascals by myself." He said that he would go with her. Izzy had fed fourteen workers the day before and ten this morning.

At the grocery store in town both adults told Homer and Annie that they were to get no sweets; it would spoil their appetites and besides it was bad for their teeth. But Clara could not resist getting them two bars of chocolate-covered ice cream on a stick. Clara paid for the ten sacks of groceries with a check and said that Izzy would give her a check.

At the ranch house Clara insisted that Homer and Annie take a nap. Izzy fed George a piece of one of the apple pies she had baked. After he brought in the groceries, she would not let him help her any more. He felt useless. The newspaper editor called from town, and he told them everything he knew about the fire. Which was not much.

He went down to the barn and climbed the ladder into the hayloft. From the large open loading window he could see far to the east and south. Mostly he saw smoke moving with a slow wind. It looked like the fire had come half a mile onto the ranch land over toward the Old Place. Once the uneven air currents lifted the smoke and showed him for a minute a black hillside three or four miles away.

He was wondering whether he should drive out to the east when he came back to the house, halfway wondering also whether he could do something for Izzy. Clara, Homer, and Annie wanted to drive out toward the fire. He guessed that they would get in Izzy's way while she cooked. Also he could stay at a safe distance and stay out of the firefighters' way. He agreed.

They piled into the old Pontiac. For some reason Annie wanted him to go the same way that he had decided to go, along the wagon road toward the Old Place. When they came to the turnoff leading to the tenant farms, she said, "Let's go straight on, Uncle George."

He pulled out onto a ridge and they stepped out of the air-conditioned car into the heat. Now they could smell the smoke but could not see much other than smoke. Annie said, "Let's go on, Uncle George."

He figured that their curiosity would never be satisfied until they had seen some fire. There was none behind them or to either side, so they would be safe. He drove on toward the Old Place. There had been a clear field of about sixty acres just beyond the early house and outbuildings, and it had never grown back with mesquite or other brush but had always been overgrown with broomweeds, sunflowers, and such. The fire had come into that abandoned field. He stopped at about where the front yard of the early house had been, and they got out. The acrid smell of burning weeds was strong, though not much smoke blew toward them.

Suddenly he saw that the sagging gray barn, a hundred yards away, had caught fire on the other side. It was all that was left of the Old Place. Annie made a little meaningless cry and started running toward the barn. Clara screamed at her.

He yelled, "Stop, Annie! Come back!"

Homer started loping after her.

George easily caught the nearly grown boy and pushed him back. Homer fell down.

He could not catch the child. She scrambled through a broken place in the rotten plank fence, and he had to climb over. The crib at the other end of the barn was blazing, but the harness shed at the near end was not. Smoke swirled through the dozen stalls between so that he could hardly see.

The stalls had upright members which supported the roof and split rails dividing them horizontally, a feed trough at the end of each. He searched desperately in the smoke, his eyes, nose, and throat burning. Then he saw her in the end stall, climbing the ladder of rails toward the eaves of the roof.

When he got beneath her, he could see that she was grasping into the cubicle between the top plate of the wall and the roof. Hot smoke and even some flame touched her. He pulled her down into his arms.

He kicked a couple of rotten planks loose from the fence and carried her through. Out of immediate danger, he set her on her feet. Her hair was singed, the blue ribbon curled up from the heat. One puff sleeve of her dress was burned. In one hand she gripped a roll of paper that had both ends burned off, in the other hand a smaller roll that was only burned on one corner.

She looked at him with bleary eyes and with a little smile on her dirty face. "My will got burned, but my Great-great-Papa must of given me another will. It was our secret place."

Homer came up and helped the best he could to lead her back to the car. Clara had evidently understood that she could help most by staying back near the car.

Annie handed George the smaller roll of paper and asked, "What does my new will say?"

After Clara had picked the child up in her arms, he read: "Codicil. To Gentle Annie. A couple of things I forgot. You know the still, shallow water where the cattails grow? There the water-skating spiders and snake doctors live. They seem like magic. They are yours, with love from your Great-great-Papa Woodstock."

She clapped her hands and said, "Water-skating spiders and snake doctors."

They took her back to the ranch house. Clara gave her a bath and found only minor burns on her forehead and one arm. They took her into town to a doctor, who found not much wrong and put on two bandages. George had cash to pay the twenty-dollar fee. Clara insisted on going to the drygoods store, where she bought the child a new dress as much like the old one as possible. She also bought a straw cowboy hat for Homer.

Late that afternoon Johnny brought in the four hands who had been working for him and six who had been working for the Pendleton. They had not saved the old barn, but finally had stopped all the fire on Woodstock land. They were a dirty, hot crew. Izzy fed them and cooled them with a half dozen pitchers of iced tea. Johnny did not take the men back out, but set up two-man patrols to watch through the night.

George had looked up the word "codicil" in the big dictionary in the library room. It was a supplement to a will. He lay in bed wondering. The child had said, "Papa must of made me a new will." She had not known it was there. That meant that Papa had been on the place since he left the nursing home. Homer had maybe heard it, but would not be able to see the meaning. Clara had not heard it and evidently believed that both rolls of paper had been hidden by Papa and Annie a year or more ago.

He remembered thinking once before that one person on earth might know the ranch land better than Johnny. Or more than once he had thought it and pushed the idea away.

Papa could have come to the ranch only a day or so, then gone on somewhere else. It was hard to imagine his chasing around over the country as that damned detective Dobbs seemed to think. Who could tell what might be in the mind, what could seem important to an old man? Maybe it would be as easy to figure out Homer's mind.

It was true that Papa seemed to be here in some way, in this house, on this land, talking and dealing with the people here. No question that Johnny had handled the fire just as the old man would have, as if Papa were whispering in his ear. Izzy had said something along that same line. George determined not to say anything about his various wonderings to anybody else.

Johnny was out at dawn in his pickup, inspecting the fire front. He reported that everything was out, except here and there an old tree or tree stump. A call to the Pendleton told him that they were in the same shape and were sending all the extra hands back to town. All it would take now was an inspection once or twice a day till every smouldering spark was dead.

The Woodstock had been lucky to lose so little grass. George headed back east.

CHAPTER FIFTEEN

A Tale Told by an Idiot

IN the first week of August he could not keep the approaching meeting of the heirs out of his mind. Sitting in the small crowded office at the shop, trying to figure a bid or trying to make a working sketch, he found himself mulling over arguments on both sides of questions about the ranch. He would force himself to pay attention to the task at hand, only to lose the concentration five minutes later.

Walter had put himself in a position to run the show by bringing in his own lawyers and accountants, but that didn't mean that his scheme for making a playground for rich people had to be accepted. In fact, Walter might find that his take-charge attitude didn't get him anything but trouble.

It seemed certain that there would be arguments. Irma and her preacher son Wilbur would make a hard-sell pitch for the Christian retreat and the Noah's Ark. They would try to show that it was a big sin to disagree with them. They wouldn't give up easy. Thank God her son Larry was probably doing his thing in Toledo or somewhere.

Clarence and his son Frank probably would not press their plan, even though the idea of an oil company might be a good proposition. Clara usually agreed with the last person she had talked to in a matter like this, and the others would all try to get her vote. But no telling what Ed Bender would advise her: maybe that the ranch should set up a service to do income taxes for people who run hardware stores.

George felt some guilt about Izzy and Johnny. They ought to have a place somewhere, somehow. If push came to shove, he would insist that they should be paid for their years of work. Or better, that the ranch, or part of it, should continue with Izzy and Johnny in charge. In fact, he would violate Walter's warning about lawyers and see that those two had some local lawyers to advise them. Johnny had made good sense about the two hundred young cows adapted to the land.

He remembered a kind of humorous scandal about Izzy four or five years ago. The woman could not keep from gardening and could not stand to let vegetables go to waste, so she canned all that she could not get people to eat. But the cellar shelves filled up with jars, pints, quarts, half-gallons, of English peas, sweet corn, jelly, jam, hominy, peach pickles; and her storage cans and boxes filled with dried black eyed peas and such. Also her big freezer was full. She had no place to put her stuff, so she gave Johnny orders, and together they hauled three pickup loads into town: seven hundred jars, including canned chili, ninety long sacks of pork sausage, several wooden boxes of salt pork, and a pickup load of frozen chicken meat. The local Salvation Army and Red Cross representatives could not handle it all and had to ship most of it into the nearest cities. Papa and Johnny teased her about it, but as soon as she had her shelves cleared, she went right out and started planting more garden.

George figured it could be that he should go in with Clarence and maybe Clara and hire a lawyer of their own to offset whatever schemes Walter might try to pull. He actually could not imagine what all might be involved, and whether the question of Papa being dead or alive might be important.

He wanted to avoid arguments or any kind of hassle,

but also he did not intend to be run over. If there was any way for him to take a hundred thousand dollars out of the estate, he meant to speak up. If he made anybody mad, that was just too bad. He had a right to the stake that Papa had understood and approved. Sometimes he asked himself: Why in the world can't people learn some skill or trade and become good at it, some work that is useful, and figure out a better way to do it and take satisfaction in hard work, instead of trying to twist other people around their finger all the time?

Helen had agreed to go with him. She actually liked Izzy and Johnny and some of the Woodstock kin, but really did not care to be around others of them. She was concerned about what clothes to take.

"Well, it's only three days," George pointed out.

"But we don't know who all will be there and if there might even be a funeral service or something. I know Walter's wife and that oldest daughter of his; they will be dressed up to kill."

"Yeah. And chattering about going to Paris and Acapulco. We don't have to keep up with them. They'll be the ones out of place. If they think we're Texas hicks, that's their problem."

He told her to buy whatever she needed, or thought she needed. It was a new idea that there would be more than his two brothers and two sisters there, but it was a possibility. In fact, some of them might bring family members as if to add weight to their own projects.

He did not want to get stuck with the job of picking people up at the airport and hauling them west, unless maybe Clarence. He was ready when Irma called from Atlanta. Would he have room for her in his car? And Wilbur and his daughter and one grandson. And probably Larry and his fiancee wanted to come. They didn't mind being a little crowded. George said he was sorry, but Helen was going and he might be obliged to carry Clarence and didn't know how many Clarence might bring with him.

She wondered how they were going to be able to make connections. He said they could fly into Dallas-Fort Worth or Wichita Falls or Amarillo or Lubbock or Abilene and rent a car. Or take a bus. A busline ran through Woodstock. He was sorry.

Clarence never did call, and George felt guilty about it. He thought about calling the youngest brother and offering a ride, but decided to leave well enough alone.

He did not look forward to the meeting, to the hassle. And he felt uncertain about what had happened in the past and what might be settled in the future. Surely the queen thing with Izzy was the truth, and who would have guessed such a strange thing? As for the possibility that Johnny was actually Papa's illegitimate son, the fact that Irma insisted that it was impossible—that didn't mean a thing. Irma was as big a dingbat as Clara. In fact, he determined that if he ever heard Clara called a dingbat again, he would not laugh but would defend her. The thing about the meeting was the uncertainty. Had any of the others got the idea that maybe Papa pulled part of Dead Cowbones Bluff down on himself? The future of the ranch was as uncertain as the past; some of the heirs were going to be dissatisfied with whatever was decided. There would be some kind of compromise.

He concluded that there are some things which are never settled, about what has happened and what is going to happen.

On the afternoon of the fourteenth of August, when he turned off the highway onto the ranch land, Helen asked why he had not taken the good graded road. He said, "Just wanted to look at the land. This was the road when us kids used to ride horseback to school." There had been some summer showers, and things looked greener than they had a few weeks ago.

She asked, "Why didn't you go on to college like Walter and Clarence and Irma did?"

He could not think of a good answer, but said, "Had other things to do, like fight a war. Why don't you ask Walter why he didn't go into combat like Clarence and me and Clara's husband did?"

They laughed. They laughed again at the prairie dog town, at the stiff little devils standing straight up beside their mounds.

Six or eight cars were parked around the ranch house, besides Johnny's pickup and a new Jeep he had bought. Inside the yard fence, Izzy had a half dozen big bushes blooming a ridiculous pink for this time of year in this climate.

George realized that the place was not really a madhouse; it only seemed so with all the people in a usually quiet place. The old dog, Gabe, was peering out from under the smokehouse, and George sympathized with his hiding. Clarence had brought Frank and his wife and kids. Clara Bender's sons Ed and Fred were there with their wives Maybelle and Pauline, with probably some kids besides Homer and Annie. Walter's wife and a son and daughter had come with evidently several more offspring. Irma Abbott had brought Wilbur and Irene and their kids; somehow her son Larry had shown up with Bonnie.

George could not identify half of them. They were every size and shape, dressed in every way imaginable. Helen quickly found Clara and began talking with her.

On the back gallery Bonnie called out, "Hey, Babe, here's your dear old Uncle George." She was barefooted and in a sunsuit.

Larry came out of one of the screen doors. "Hey, man, you going to call the cops on me? Go ahead on. Call the cops." The young man still had his bushy hair and beard but was dressed in cleaner clothes.

George did not answer. The two actually seemed hopped up on something.

Larry laughed. "He don't know where we're coming from. Listen, Old Dude. Last time I seen you, you was going to call the police. Then you tried to like send me to Toledo. When my old lady gets to running this place, I may call the cops on you."

"You'll send Uncle George to Toledo, won't you, Babe?"

He went through the kitchen door and on into the bathroom, where he had meant to go, determined to stay away from those two as much as possible. In the hall five or six men and women who looked vaguely familiar called him "Uncle George."

Back outside he saw Homer and Annie wandering around together. They did not seem to know what to do with so many new kinfolks all at once. Gabe dashed out from under the smokehouse to join them. Annie did not show any scar from the burns on her arm and forehead.

Down past the first windmill, halfway to the barn, a youngster about sixteen was strolling around, or strutting. He was carrying a portable radio, blaring rock music. Unlike Homer and Annie, he did not stay back from the others because he was timid, but because he wanted to call attention to himself. His head was shaved except for a tuft sticking up in the center from front to back. Around his neck, he wore glass beads, over his chest, a leather vest. He had a large red patch on the seat of his blue jeans. He did not look like he had spent much time in the sun, and George thought, without much sorrow, that the kid would probably get his head sunburned. The kid was undoubtedly one of his grandnephews, but he could not guess what brother or sister could have produced such a grandchild. In fact, he had seen such funny looking humans on television, but had never quite believed it.

Izzy was working like a beaver, with some help from

Clara and Helen. After supper they put sheets on the twelve bunks in the bunkhouse. It was agreed that the women and children would sleep in the house on beds and pallets, and the men would sleep in the bunkhouse. George put his small bag on the bunk at the end. The long room was like a barracks. It had a toilet and wash basin but no shower or bath. An evaporative cooler blew a nice breeze down the length of the room and out a screen door at the front.

Some of the crowd went into town to sleep in the homes of Clara's two sons. Walter evidently went to his suite in a motel.

That night Homer created a disturbance. It was thought later that he was mixed up because three or four kids were parked in his bed. An old kerosene lantern had been hanging unused in the smokehouse for years. Somehow Homer got oil in it and got it lighted and went around scaring people who were trying to sleep.

George saw the lighted lantern through a screened bunkhouse window. It was moving around in the yard and on the back gallery. He thought it might be Johnny taking care of something.

When he was almost asleep he began to hear faint sounds from the house: screams, yells, laughter. The sounds would stop and then seem to repeat at another room in the house. He thought they must be having a lot of fun. The commotion went on for half an hour.

He woke up when the trouble started in the bunkhouse. Someone down at the front end said, "What is it? What the hell?" He could see the pale yellow light of a lantern and a hulk of a person who seemed to be shuffling along to the next bunk in a clumsy way. The light stopped, and some man said, "What? Damn! Get out of here!" The light proceeded from bunk to bunk, getting responses of fear and anger.

Twenty or thirty feet from his bunk, George saw the

intruder clearly. It was Homer, holding the old lantern forward, peering at a sleeping man, maybe Frank, Clarence's son. "What's the matter? Dammit! Who are you?" Homer's eyes looked bright in the yellow light and his face looked like a bad dream. George rolled out of the bunk and began to put his trousers on.

At that moment Clara came in the door with a flashlight. She was swishing along in a bulky gray nightgown, her bare feet showing beneath it. "Homer," she said, "come on, honey. Let Granny have the lantern." The youngster peered at George a second, then gave her the kerosene light and went out the door with her.

Several in the bunkhouse commented before going back to sleep. "You know, that kid looked like a devil." "That idiot will burn this place down." "He looked like a dead man." "Hell, those eyes! They look right through you."

George got the idea, for no reason he could name, that Homer was looking for Papa, believing that somehow, in such a strange gathering of Woodstocks, Papa must be hidden among them.

The following day, the awaited August the fifteenth, was partly cloudy but hot. Much of the day was spent chatting, eating, drinking iced tea, waiting.

George had a long talk with Clarence, who had spoken on the phone a few days before with the private investigator Dobbs. It seemed the detective was now in El Paso, hot on the trail of an elderly man who looked like he might have been a Texas rancher. Dobbs was wondering whether his quarry might have gone on to Tucson or Santa Fe. Clarence was aggravated with the man for his continual demands for photographs. Dobbs was in the process of having a police artist make up a sketch of what

Franklin Woodstock must look like, as if Papa were a wanted criminal.

Walter called two or three times that day from town. Apparently he wanted to make sure his two brothers and two sisters were present and waiting at the ranch. He had some consulting and planning to do with lawyers and accountants. He would come out in due time.

In the afternoon Clarence and Johnny gave some of the grandkids and great-grandkids rides on Old Baldy and Old Hickory. Some of the kids had never been on a horse and were delighted. Old Gabe stuck his tail between his legs and whined and even barked at the strange kids who had invaded his world.

Late in the afternoon Walter showed up with two other men carrying briefcases. Izzy was feeding everyone supper in shifts, happy as a lark to be mothering such a bunch. Most of the great grandchildren were stuffing themselves with dewberry cobbler covered with ice cream.

Little Annie was begging George to take her for a ride in the new Jeep which Johnny had bought. "Later," he kept telling her. "I have to listen to your Great-uncle, Walter, first."

"Please, Uncle George. Pretty please! You will really take me and Homer for a ride, won't you?" She had been running around the Jeep, jumping in it, pretending to drive it, for an hour.

Her mother, Pauline, approached and said, "You are going to get into trouble, young lady, if you do not settle down."

But her grandmother, Clara, as usual trying to put in her two cents, said, "Oh, let her play with the new Jeep. George won't mind driving her around some. He's a good driver."

"I promise to take you and Homer for a ride later," he

said. "Right now your Great-uncle Walter wants me in the big room." The sun was already touching a bank of clouds low on the western horizon when he went inside.

Walter was having trouble taking control of the situation in the big library room. His two brothers and two sisters were there, but also a dozen others, sitting or standing. He said, "If I could have your attention, please." The two lawyers, one a puzzled, well-dressed stranger, one a local man wearing Levis and an old shirt, stood near him, as if backing him up.

"Our main purpose at this time," Walter said, "is to agree to have our father declared dead, legally, though it is a sad and difficult step. If we, the five of us, vote that it is a necessary step, then we can proceed with the proper legal strategy to approach the probate court and other authorities. I'm sure that Papa would want us to cooperate."

They were mumbling around the room, paying scant attention to him, talking about the weather and even the latest television programs.

"Listen," Walter said. "I am going to insist that we get a few things settled here tonight. Some of us have gone out of our way to gather here, and it is necessary to have the five immediate descendants agree so that we can appoint one of the five to take care of these matters."

Johnny stepped forward with obvious reluctance. He said, "We have to keep the two hundred young cows I talked to you and everybody about. I know Papa wanted us to."

Walter ignored him and raised his voice. "Our biggest problem at this moment is too many people in this room. I am going to ask that everyone leave except Clara, George, Clarence, Irma, myself, and our counsel. We need to have some degree of order so that we can vote concerning the question of having our father declared legally deceased. Then we should vote on an executor and instruct our attorneys."

No one was leaving. In fact, Homer was creating a disturbance, pushing Johnny back toward the lawyers. The clumsy youth said loudly, "Show my papers now!" He was thrusting two pieces of paper into the Chicano's hand. "Now time! Show papers!"

The unusual behavior caused the room to become quiet. Johnny said to Walter, "I still want to know if you agree to keep the two hundred young cows. Papa and I worked a long time. I know he would want it."

"I don't know what you are talking about, young man. I have asked you and everyone who doesn't belong here to please leave the room and allow us to transact important business."

"Show my papers, Johnny! Now!"

Walter had put his hands on his hips.

Still with some reluctance, Johnny handed the two papers to the local lawyer and backed away. The man, in his casual gray sweater, looked at the papers with an amused chuckle.

Then he began to frown. Then he began to laugh a silly laugh. "My God Almighty!" He looked back and forth from one paper to the other. He kept them in suspense for some interminable seconds with a foolish half laugh. "Walter, I know these signatures. Seen them a hundred times. Even the notary publics. These are machine copies right out of the County Clerk's office. I'm afraid you don't have a quorum here for a vote on the estate, Walter. According to the community property laws of Texas, the half owner is not present. I believe she's in yonder in the kitchen washing dishes."

In the hushed room they were all trying to digest the new information, whatever it was. The lawyer went on. "This is a marriage license for Franklin Woodstock and Miss Isabel Maria Zavalla. The ceremony was read a few days later by the Reverend Biggs, who served for years as pastor of the First Baptist Church. I know all these signatures. These are true copies. This other paper is a birth certificate dated ten months later for a male infant, Juan Franklin Woodstock, delivered by old Doc Herndon."

They began to buzz with talk in the room. Walter and the two lawyers began a three-way argument. George drew back to the double door where the main hall joined the library. He saw Homer and Annie there in the half-lit hall, arguing. Homer said, "Papa here too."

She said, "No!" and stamped her small slipper, acting like a Shirley Temple doll. "You told me, Homer! You know you did."

But Homer said, "He also right here. Don't you see?" His arm stretched out toward the old fireplace and the thousands of books and the chattering, gossiping crowd. "Please see Papa here."

"No! I say, No!"

They glared at each other. Then their faces turned to pleading, and she reached out to hold his arm in a gesture of forgiveness. Homer kissed her clumsily on the top of the head.

She saw him and said, "Oh, Uncle George, it's real dark already, and remember your promise. Please. We want to go for a ride. You promised."

He could not deny the promise.

Halfway out to the Jeep he saw that Johnny was ahead of him with Homer and Annie. If they did not need him to drive, why was he going? A strange kind of reluctance prevented him from turning back immediately—to that stuffy, vain, irresponsible, hectic nonsense back there in the big room. His arithmetic mind, as if ignoring his will, was saying: Izzy and Johnny own seven-twelfths of the ranch. Then the way they got into the Jeep left him no choice, unless he wanted to make some kind of an issue out of the matter.

Annie scrambled nimbly into the front beside the driver's seat without opening the door. Homer, with custom-ary awkwardness, managed to labor into the seat behind her. Johnny, in that strange competent way that did not match his sturdy form, vaulted into the other back seat.

Johnny said, "The key is in the switch."

Of course the damned key was in the switch. Some people took pride in locking things and leaving the key handy, in case somebody, anybody, wanted to borrow something.

When he got in, the girl said, "We want to go out near Dead Cowbones Bluff." Then she glanced at him and said in a matter-of-fact, peremptory manner, "Please." Then she turned her small white face forward, her chin set. As if she had said, You have your instructions; now execute.

It was as if she knew, they knew, that he did not want to be among those back in the big room. She was not so much a dictator as a spokesman. He backed the open vehicle into the driveway. The steering was a little tight, and when he took the wagon road west, the suspension seemed stiff. The damned Jeep would probably climb over the Rocky Mountains but was not built for luxury.

The headlights looked dim because of the moonlight coming through thin drifting clouds. The moon was bright enough to leave shadows by every clump of scrub brush; it molded and exaggerated the contours of the prairie. He drove carefully, turning slightly over on the sod where a stone or an exposed root lay in the wagon tracks. But they did not seem to feel the jolts. The three passengers could not have made up any plan, yet they seemed in a determined, serene conspiracy, in which he had no choice.

A hundred yards ahead the lights of the Jeep picked up the dark form of a dog or a coyote, maybe a wolf. The form stopped directly in the center between the lighter colored wagon tracks. For an instant the animal's eyes reflected back the light of the headlamps, and one could almost see ears erect, pointing at the intrusion of the Jeep. Then the form casually turned and trotted into the small hummocks of bunch grass and brush, to be lost in the myriad shadows.

At the fence of the west section he took the brief right hand detour and rumbled over the pipes of the cattle-guard. Johnny, the efficient, always put the cattle-guard, for a tractor or a truck, on the right and the troublesome gate, for a saddle horse or a team, on the left—if a person were going away from the ranch house; it was opposite if you were coming home. The impression of that efficiency fitted ironically into the feeling of the vast, non-human moonlit night.

The crude road led gently upward toward Dead Cow-bones Bluff. Annie announced, "Go near the edge and stop. Please."

There was no question that other vehicles had come near the drop-off, so there was no danger. He remembered the place clearly; they were a safe distance from the point that was crumbling. He stopped fifteen feet from the edge and set the brake. And looked. And waited.

They got out slowly, the three of them. They squatted or knelt on the flat sandstone outcrop, Annie and Homer and Johnny, looking out. George could see out there a ways, in the pink bare alkaline soil, places where the bones and fossils had washed away from the bluff and lay half buried, their exposed bleached patterns white under the moon. The scene was as solemn as a funeral.

It must have been on impulse that the girl shouted, "Papa!" for she immediately clapped her hands over her mouth and looked at her two companions. She recovered and spoke almost as loud, but in a stage whisper. "We hear you out there, Great-great Papa. Thank you. Come back to see us all the time. We will not say goodbye. We will hear you."

Homer said something in a lower voice almost like a prayer. It sounded like Latin.

It may have been that when Johnny spoke in a loud

hushed whisper, he was trying to catch the spirit of the young girl, for he tried to use the Spanish of his earliest childhood. "Hasta la vista, Padre! Otras mañanas!"

Their voices disturbed some kind of large bird which evidently had been roosting in the broken face of the cliff. It sprang out, only a vague movement in the dark, but flapping vigorously. It rose and circled over them. George thought it might be a hawk. Or an owl. Maybe a vulture. Or even an eagle, resting on that flyway between the Wichita Mountains and the Big Bend country. Though they could not see it, the swish of wings whispered as the bird circled over them in the night sky.

The child in her romantic innocence was looking up and her voice became as soft as the beating of wings in air. "Thank you for the water skating spiders and the snake doctors."